Contents

MIDWINTER

MAEVE HENRY

Mammoth

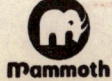

First published in Great Britain in 1997 by Mammoth
an imprint of Reed International Books Ltd
Michelin House, 81 Fulham Road, London SW3 6RB
and Auckland, Melbourne, Singapore and Toronto

Copyright © 1997 Maeve Henry

The right of Maeve Henry to be identified as the author
of this work has been asserted by her in accordance with
the Copyright, Designs and Patents Act 1988

ISBN 0 7497 2593 1

10 9 8 7 6 5 4 3 2 1

A CIP catalogue record for this book is available
from the British Library

Phototypeset by Intype London Ltd
Printed in Great Britain by Cox & Wyman Ltd, Reading, Berkshire

This paperback is sold subject to the condition
that it shall not, by way of trade or otherwise,
be lent, resold, hired out, or otherwise circulated
without the publisher's prior consent in any form
or binding or cover other than that in which
it is published and without a similar condition
including this condition being imposed
on the subsequent purchaser.

For Simone

Prologue

In a distant time and place, cradled between the great forest and the sea, lies the land of Rossendale. It has been ruled by the Ortellus family from their castle for longer than anyone knows, but for hundreds of years, ever since Lord Jago Ortellus set the Sword above his chair in the great hall, the men of Rossendale have been fierce fighters, setting out to sea to plunder neighbouring islands for gold and cattle. No one knows for sure where the Sword came from, or the secret of its fine craftsmanship, but no other sword in the land has ever rivalled it for the beauty and trueness of its blade. Some stories say a fisher lad found it washed up on the beach, and others that it was brought by a merchant from an unknown land and paid for with all the precious stones in the country. What is sure is that it has been handed down from father to son on the death-bed of each Lord, and that its possession is the sign of authority over Rossendale.

But before the coming of the Sword there had been another way of ruling. People had looked to the great forest for learning and wisdom, and the young heirs of Rossendale rode into its dark depths to be taught magic by the green people living there. Their adventures were recorded in the Chronicles, but for centuries the stories were unheeded, mouldering alongside other old books in the castle library. Few even remembered their existence on the day when Thomas Ortellus discovered them.

It was his eleventh birthday. His tutor, an old man called Dr Castang, was Keeper of the Chronicles, and instead of the usual dull lessons in the schoolroom, he gave Thomas the freedom of the library. While Dr Castang toiled away behind a pile of books, scratching notes in a ledger with a huge quill pen, Thomas wandered among the shelves, almost afraid to disturb the dust and silence. There were books ranged in heavy cases from floor to ceiling, books chained to desks and books locked away in old worm-eaten chests. Thomas took down one shabby leather-bound volume after another, turning the pages with growing excitement. He found small salt-stained journals written by mariners telling of voyages to far-off lands and of the strange wonders seen along the way. He skimmed through volumes devoted to alchemy and astronomy, with arcane diagrams marked out on thick parchment pages. But when he reached the Chronicles he forgot all about the rest.

On that first day he read about Lord Isaac Ortellus, who lived seven years in the forest as a bear under enchantment, and about Lord Ozias Ortellus, his son, who went hunting by moonlight with the green people, deep in the forest's heart. What wonders he saw, or what strange beasts he chased no one could say, for he would never speak of it, but a spell of his for calming storms was recorded in the Chronicles. When he reached it, Thomas broke off and looked over his shoulder at Dr Castang. Small sharp eyes were watching him over the pile of books. Thomas picked up the heavy volume and opened his mouth to speak, but Dr Castang shook his head, and began scratching away at his ledger in nervous haste. Thomas understood then that he must keep his questions to himself.

After that day, Dr Castang often took Thomas to the library, sitting in silence while the boy read and wondered. Thomas learnt about princes who could take the shapes of birds and animals at will, and others who found strange secrets in the stones, relics of an age before there were men. Silently, and a little guiltily, he began to question why the men of Rossendale had forgotten the forest, and why they thought fighting their enemies the only worthwhile adventure. More guiltily still, he began to memorise some of the spells and words of power transcribed in the Chronicles. He was drawn to the idea of the forest by a strange and powerful attraction. It filled his dreams and the pauses of his waking life, yet in the Rossendale of his time it was a place to be feared and hated. He knew he had no right to dabble in magic. As his father's heir, he must learn to be a swordsman and a battle-leader, the most fearless and daring in the raids. He kept his knowledge hidden, dreaming of a time when he would be free to follow his own path.

Thomas did not know that very soon he would need every spell and story, and all his courage and wit, for a quest to save Rossendale more urgent than any adventure in the Chronicles.

One

Darkness was falling on the battlements of Ortellus Castle, and the snow had begun again. Thomas Ortellus stood, arms raised and body turned to present the narrowest target to his enemy. At his feet lay the sword hooked out of his hand by his father's stick.

'Slovenly,' Lord Ortellus pronounced with absolute authority. 'Wouldn't do credit to the rawest farm-boy. When I was eleven I went out on my first raid and here are you at – what age, boy?'

'Twelve,' Thomas muttered.

'Speak up, can't you? Here are you, at the ripe age of twelve, with years of practice and the honour of the family to maintain, unable to perform the simplest . . .' He broke off, shaking his head as if words were inadequate to describe his feelings. 'What do you think, Captain? You wouldn't like to take him on, would you?'

The Captain of the Guard, standing a little behind him, smiled diplomatically. 'My Lord, it is very cold, and the poor boy's hands must be nearly numb. It's not a fair test of his ability. He dropped the sword through cold, not clumsiness.'

Lord Ortellus snorted. 'That excuse wouldn't save him if he was fighting a raider.'

Thomas lifted his chin, willing his face not to show his feelings. 'I'd make a good look-out, at least. My eyes are sharp, and I don't get bored with watching. I wish you'd let me join the watch, if you don't think I'm good enough for the guard yet.'

His father looked at him. Then he laughed, shortly and without humour. 'You? You'd better stay in the schoolroom till you've learnt how to hold a sword.'

The two men moved on, talking briskly. Thomas followed after a moment, trailing behind them unhappily. An hour ago he had been pleased and excited when his father fetched him from the schoolroom to inspect the guard posts. It didn't happen very often. For a while things had gone well. Thomas had been able to answer nearly all his father's questions, and had given his salutes and passwords smartly. But his father could never rest until he found some reason to be dissatisfied.

'He knew that lunge wasn't fair,' Thomas muttered to himself. 'He could see I hadn't finished taking up position.'

Ahead of him, his father and the captain had stopped just under the little tower, too absorbed in their discussion to care about the flakes of snow the wind was driving into their faces. Their hands sketched rapid diagrams in the air against the dying light. Thomas stood at a little distance, watching his father with a pride that hurt. The lines of his handsome face were a little blurred with fat, and there was grey in his fair hair, but he remained a man of extraordinary physical presence. He had been Lord of Rossendale for more than ten years, defending the country and leading the raids with a success unprecedented in recent history. Thomas was a thin, wary-looking boy, with his father's fair hair but none of his father's grace as yet. He was jealous of the captain, standing so close to his father, saying something that made him laugh. Thomas had had a dream once in which he had killed the captain and taken his place.

The darkness was growing and the lights began to glimmer in the harbour village. The wind rose, buffeting Thomas's face until his ears ached and his skin burned. He could hardly feel the snow falling any more. His body was stiff with cold and his ears were full of the roaring of the wind; his whole head was full of it. Only his eyes were still working, scanning the open sea. From the black slab of the harbour wall his eyes travelled across the dark to the beacon at Seal Point. Suddenly he peered forward, straining his eyes till they began to smart and water.

There was something, surely, an unexpected shape against the needle rocks north of the light? Thomas could not believe it. He looked behind him. His father and the captain talked on, absorbed. He looked back at the shadow. A fishing boat, he told himself; a straggler returning late. But already the fine hair on the back of his neck had risen, rejecting that explanation. His heart began to beat fast as he waited for the boat to cross the line of the beacon. He recognised the slim curve of the prow and saw the carved snarl of the figurehead. He turned to his father, took a step, opened his mouth to speak, when a voice from the tower above him bellowed, 'Raiders!'

As his father and the captain looked wildly round, the great bell began to clamour, summoning all the men to assemble in the castle yard.

* * *

The women sat waiting for news, the strain of anxiety visible on every face. Thomas waited with them. Normally he was glad to spend the long winter evenings in his mother's room, where there was always a fire and where the women of the household gathered to talk. Tonight he sat on the edge of his seat and listened to the noise of soldiers stamping along the stone passageway outside and tried to guess what was happening. Someone would certainly be riding up the headland to light the beacons and alert the watchmen up and down the coast. Thomas looked down at the glow of the firelight on his hands and imagined for a moment that he was there. He felt the terror and exhilaration of racing through the dark with the raiders ashore behind him; then abruptly the life went out of his fantasy. It was too far from the truth. As soon as the alarm had sounded, his father had ordered him inside and out of the way. He hadn't even had a chance to tell him that he had been the first to see the raiders.

For a long time there was silence in the room, broken only by the noise outside and by the persistent exhausted cough of Lady Ortellus. Her sister, Thomas's Aunt Marina, paused in the restless pleating and unpleating of the folds of her dress to speak.

'Well, we don't know for certain that it's them. It's easy to make a mistake in the dark. I think we may all look very foolish in the morning.'

'Some of us look foolish now.' It was the dry voice of Margaret Claypole.

'Whatever do you mean?' Marina demanded rather stridently. She feared and disliked the old woman, though she could not have told why.

Margaret Claypole smiled. 'Don't you think we should have expected something out of the ordinary after what happened last spring?'

Thomas looked up thoughtfully. Unlike Marina he trusted Margaret, and he realised she was right. Last spring the raiders had departed from their normal course, and it had brought them considerable success. Instead of starting the season by harrying the remoter farms and gradually working towards the castle, they had sailed into Ortellus Harbour at full strength on the first spring tide. Before the men of the castle had time to prepare an attack, the raiders had set fire to most of the ships at anchor under the castle wall. A wild attempt to storm the castle had been easily repulsed, but the islanders had escaped to raid the countryside with only half a fleet to pursue them. It had taken the summer and most of the autumn to replace the lost ships, but the autumn raids, when at last they came, had been savagely successful for Rossendale. The men of the castle had expected a quieter spring than usual as a result.

'But there is no reason for them to come now,' persisted Aunt Marina. 'They never have before. The tides make it so difficult.'

'They broke the pattern last spring,' said Margaret Claypole. 'When people start to change, there's no telling what their new habits will be.'

'Spoken with all the wisdom of hindsight,' said Lady Ortellus rather spitefully.

Thomas glanced at his mother and looked away again quickly before she could catch him doing it.

'But what can they want at this time of year?' asked another of the women. 'It's winter. There's nothing to steal.'

Margaret Claypole laughed low and maliciously. It was such an unexpected sound that everybody stared.

Then Aunt Marina began to speak in a high hysterical voice. 'What if they've landed all along the coast? Perhaps they got to the beacons and killed the watchmen before they could be lit. They may be everywhere and this is the last place. And what if they have someone here to open the gate for them?'

Lady Ortellus made an impatient gesture and started to speak, then broke into a terrible fit of coughing. The dry exhausted sound of it wrung Thomas's heart. She beat her hand irritably on the arm of her chair until the fit was over, then she said, 'Margaret pretends to know more than any of us. So tell us, Margaret, why have the raiders come now? What do they want?'

Margaret Claypole smiled. 'What did they want last spring, my Lady? Only the thing we could not give them. Disturbance breeds disturbance, some would say.'

Lady Ortellus started. Then she said in her voice of ice, 'Go to bed, Thomas.'

Thomas stood up automatically, but Margaret Claypole reached out and seized his arm with fierce bony fingers. 'Why must he go?' she demanded. 'Will you make him Lord of Rossendale without ever telling him the truth? When are you going to tell him about Midwinter?'

Pandemonium broke out among the women. One woman started talking randomly about the raiders, another about what the soldiers might be doing just then. The rest made hushing noises and cast angry or frightened glances at Margaret. Over all could be heard the voice of Thomas's mother, coldly repeating her demand that he go to bed. She and Margaret were staring at each other like enemies. Thomas flushed with excitement and uncertainty.

For a moment he thought Margaret would not let him go, then she released him with a gentle push. He turned to her, but she gave a faint shake of the head. Reluctantly, Thomas crossed the circle to his mother. He kissed her on the cheek and felt the usual movement as she resisted the impulse to draw away. That knowledge was too familiar to cause him any pain. Instead he felt alarm at the feverish dry heat of her skin under his lips. She was holding herself rigid, a hand pressed against her ribs. The slightest excitement left her exhausted; the shock of the raiders coming and now this quarrel with Margaret could be dangerous.

He was searching for something to say to her, some way to express his concern, when her dark eyes met his, impatient for him to be gone. Thomas turned at once and said goodnight to the rest of the company, his glance resting longest on Margaret's sympathetic face. Then he walked, smarting, to his room.

This was in the oldest part of the castle, the north-east tower, reached by a spiral staircase rising from a corner of the great hall. It was horribly cold. Thomas sat down on his bed and pulled off his boots and his sheepskin jacket. The night wind off the sea had begun to howl round the castle and the shutters shook with the force of it. When his servant Billy came to open them in the morning the window slits would be full of snow. Thomas slid under the thick pile of blankets and furs without bothering to take off the rest of his clothes. He wanted to drift into sleep, revelling in the luxury of being warm all over, but too much had happened. Down in the harbour a dozen or more beaked ships rode the cold water. He wondered if there were any boys aboard them, keeping watch. They would not be sleeping on such a bitter night, nor the soldiers of the castle, nor his father. Perhaps the fighting had already begun. And all he could do was wait, like the women; wait and guess.

He turned over restlessly and curled into a tighter ball. He tried to remember exactly what Margaret had said just now to make his mother so angry. Disturbance breeds disturbance. Tell the truth. Midwinter. Thomas opened his eyes and stared at the dark. He realised fully for the first time that Margaret had been talking about *him*. '*Will you make him Lord of Rossendale without ever telling him the truth? When are you going to tell him about Midwinter?*'

'But I know all about Midwinter,' he murmured, confused. 'And he's got nothing to do with the raiders.'

The smallest child knew about Midwinter's dreadful crime, how he had stolen the Sword out of the great hall and fled with it into the forest. Such was the unease felt in Rossendale about the forest that no one had dared to pursue him. Yet the shame of the loss was immense. Thomas was too young to remember the shock and confusion of that time, more than ten years ago, when goldsmiths and silversmiths had been summoned from all over Rossendale and abroad to try to fashion a new sword. Nothing had been found to match the ancient workmanship and the sword case in the hall above his father's head still hung empty, like a reproach. No one spoke of the matter publicly, for the worst of it was that Midwinter was Lord Ortellus's own brother.

The strange thing was that after so long Thomas could still remember Midwinter's bony face and his rare, transforming smile. Midwinter had been no soldier. He lived for his books and his experiments, and when he left them to eat with the household, Thomas seemed to remember that he had always sat near him. His deep blue eyes, the faint gunpowdery smell of his clothes and the chemical stains on his fingers returned to the boy vividly . . . as did a disturbing sense of attraction.

Midwinter had spent many hours in the library, Thomas knew . . . Midwinter had escaped into the forest . . .

'But he was mad,' Thomas said aloud. 'He must have been, to run off with the Sword like that.'

Midwinter had lived in the room above his own, and the noise of his experiments had sometimes wakened Thomas from sleep. And now he remembered talk about his servant, a swarthy fellow called Declan, with crooked shoulders and something wrong with his speech, whom Midwinter had rescued from torment among the kitchen boys.

But that doesn't make him good, Thomas thought, turning uneasily in his bed. Midwinter was a thief, and Declan was too. When I get to the forest I'll find them and bring the Sword back.

The idea was not a new one, but perhaps because of Margaret's words, it struck him with fresh force. *I'm the only one that can get the Sword back. I'm the only one who's not afraid.*

He would set out now, in spite of the raiders and the bitter weather. He thought of his father's reaction, disbelief transformed into pride, as Thomas brought in the Sword to the sound of trumpets and laid it triumphantly before him. But then a familiar and horrifying image flashed into his mind, driving out all thought of the Sword or the raiders.

Thomas stiffened. Tall, dark-haired and shabby in his stained black clothes, Midwinter stood in a doorway, a struggling bundle in his arms. He smiled when he saw Thomas looking at him. Then he was gone.

Thomas lay still until the shock of it had left him. Then he sat up, hugging his knees, with the blankets hunched round his shoulders. He could not fix that episode in time or place; he could not be certain if it was a memory or a dream, or why it disturbed him so deeply. Eventually, he lay down again, still shaken. When he slept at last, he dreamt he was looking out across Rossendale from the castle. A single trail of footprints crossed the snow.

Two

Two days later, Thomas was sitting in the schoolroom just as if it was an ordinary day. Down in the harbour his father was parlaying with the leaders of the enemy fleet, while beside him his tutor, Dr Castang, read in a monotone from an extraordinarily dry old text called *Rhetoric*, never lifting his eyes from the page. Thomas gazed from the book to the old man's mittened hands and then longingly towards the window. From across the room, nothing could be seen but leaden sky.

He had gleaned all the news he could about the raiders, sitting quietly in corners while the women talked, or hanging around the passageways when the guards came off duty. It seemed that, like last spring, the bulk of the raiders had joined in the attack on the castle. They had taken up positions on the headland to try to cut off any communication with the rest of the country and their ships still blocked the harbour. They looked set for a long siege. Thomas hoped his father would laugh in their faces; it was ridiculous to imagine that raiders in open boats could starve out a garrison properly sheltered from the bitter cold. But the countryside was open to them, unprotected, and black smoke had already been seen rising from distant villages. So far, Lord Ortellus had simply waited, sending out scouting parties to gather information, and parlaying with the raiders every day. But no one thought it would be long before he gave the order for battle.

Dr Castang paused in his reading and took off his spectacles, holding them tightly in his right hand like a child clutching a marble. He was a dry old man with a long skinny neck and slightly protruding eyes, reminding Thomas of a creature he had seen in a book of travellers' tales, called a tortoise.

'Lord Ortellus should be back soon,' Dr Castang said abruptly. He closed the book of rhetoric and did not open another one. Thomas glanced at him in surprise. They had not finished the section they had begun, and Dr Castang was nothing if not methodical.

'This castle was last burnt to the ground two hundred and fifty years ago,' he continued. 'The Keeper at the time perished, trying to rescue manuscripts and books from the library.'

'Oh, my father wouldn't let . . .' Thomas began, trailing off when he saw the troubled look on the old man's face.

'In the Chronicles they say it happened as a punishment,' Dr Castang continued, heavily. 'Lord Raphael Ortellus abducted the daughter of the King of Sardis. He held her against her will and would not marry her. Three years later, when her brother came on a revenge raid, Raphael and his captains were stricken with a plague, too weak to lift a sword. They all died. Those whom the Prince of Sardis did not slaughter burnt to death in the castle fire.'

'Three years is a long time to wait for a revenge raid,' Thomas said, surprised.

'If we find Sardis on the map you will see . . .' but Dr Castang seemed to lose interest even as his hand moved to the pile of charts. 'If this raid is a punishment,' he said softly, as if to himself, 'we have not deserved it. We did what we did for the sake of Rossendale.'

Thomas waited for him to say more. When he was silent, he prompted him. 'What did you do, Dr Castang? Is it in the Chronicles?'

Dr Castang looked at him in shock. He put his hand to his mouth as if he had not realised he had been speaking aloud. He looked small and old and frightened. 'Promise me you won't tell. I've said more than I should. It's this business of the raiders coming, making me foolish.'

'Of course I won't tell,' Thomas said. He hardly knew what it was he might tell, even if somebody did ask him, which was unlikely.

Dr Castang smiled shakily, and shuffled his books together. But he seemed unable to leave the subject alone.

'The thing you must realise, Thomas,' he said earnestly, 'is that Midwinter was no soldier. He was like you, only much more certain of his way. All he cared about was old books, old magic. He was like a hound on a trail. He wouldn't go out on raids. He said what happened in the time before the raids was more important. And there was your father, his brother, the best soldier of his generation. No one could deny it. Your father, after all, was a born leader.'

Thomas could not take much of this in. All he really grasped was the comparison between himself and Midwinter, and it made him both excited and angry.

'What are you trying to say about me? Am I a thief? Have I refused to go on raids? I don't like old books as much as all that. I like riding and fighting and all the things my father likes. They're what I like best.'

There was a silence in which Dr Castang looked at Thomas, and Thomas slowly blushed. 'Well,' Dr Castang said at last, 'if you tell your father that, perhaps it will reassure him.' And before Thomas could find a reply, the hall bell rang slow and loud. It was time for the midday meal.

'There we are then.' Dr Castang gathered up his books with evident relief. 'Your father will be back from the parlay. No doubt he will have something to tell us all at dinner.'

They walked down to the hall together. The benches had been pulled out from the walls and the trestle tables drawn up, but the place was half empty. Many of the soldiers were on duty outside. Thomas took his seat at the foot of the carved table up on the dais, where his Aunt Marina and Margaret Claypole were already waiting. When his father entered everyone stood up and the herald at the back of the hall played a fanfare. Once his father sat down, everyone else seated themselves and the sound of voices made a hollow roar in the gloom. The windows of the hall were high and narrow and even in summer the light was limited. On a winter's noon it was as brown and thick as the soup the servants were setting in front of Thomas. He glanced at his father, sitting in silence at the head of the table, then he tore off a piece of bread and ate ravenously. The soup tasted of flour and lentils and mutton fat; it burnt the roof of his mouth, but a few spoonfuls took the edge off his hunger. Only then did he become aware of the whispered conversation going on beside him. Margaret Claypole was leaning across, talking to Dr Castang. 'I heard it from the Captain of the Guard. It's no secret. They're not asking for cattle or grain or gold. They're not even asking to be our

17

overlords, for us to pay them a tribute of money or men. They're asking for the Sword.'

Thomas's eyes followed Dr Castang's up the table towards his father. 'And what did *he* say to that?' the old man demanded eagerly.

'He said nothing.' Margaret Claypole glanced up the table herself and frowned. 'He turned his back and walked away.'

Dr Castang was delighted. 'A good answer,' he said quite loudly. 'An excellent one. He showed them his contempt and tonight he will show them their mistake.' He smiled at his own wit. 'I wish I was a soldier. I wish I was young again. The harbour stones will be red and wet when tomorrow's tide comes in.'

Margaret Claypole looked at him. 'Will they?' she said coolly. 'Then you know more than the Captain of the Guard.'

Dr Castang looked confused. 'But surely . . . of course the order may be secret, and he could hardly tell a woman . . .'

'Especially not a foolish old one?' Margaret Claypole suggested wryly. 'Most certainly he could not. But he looked shaken, Dr Castang. I did not like the way he looked. And I do not like my Lord Ortellus's silence. The worst of it is, he's got a trouble closer to home.'

Dr Castang pulled at his sleeves and coughed. 'I think, perhaps, the boy . . .'

'Oh, he's in a dream. Look at him, he notices nothing.'

But for once Margaret Claypole was wrong. Thomas stared straight ahead, trying to take in what he had heard. The raiders had made their presumptuous demand, and his father, the Lion of Rossendale, had faltered and turned away. He had not ordered an attack. He had said, and done, nothing. It made no sense. And what had Margaret meant about a trouble closer to home? Thomas had already noticed his mother's absence from the table. It wasn't unusual, but it always made him feel uneasy. Now he broke into the conversation between Margaret and Dr Castang to demand urgently, 'What's happened to my mother?'

The old woman hesitated and the doctor looked away. That told Thomas enough, but still he leant forward to hear Margaret explain. 'She's in her room, child. Either the chill she took the night the raiders came, or the shock of it . . . at any rate the fever has got worse. She was ill this morning, very ill. I doubt she'll leave her bed again. Now then, young master,' she added sharply, as Thomas pushed away his bowl and put his hands up to his hair, 'you'll finish your dinner and be grateful for it, no matter what.'

Her old brown eyes watched him reach slowly for his bowl and spoon, then let him go. But he couldn't eat. Eventually he whispered, 'Can I see her?'

'What's that?'

'I said, can I see her?'

'Not yet.' Her voice softened. 'You needn't be afraid, Thomas. You will be called before the end comes.'

Dr Castang made a faint noise of protest which Margaret Claypole rebutted in a vigorous whisper. 'He needs to know the truth. He has to be told.'

It came to Thomas through a wall of glass. He sat back, his hands gripping the sides of his chair, and he rocked himself almost imperceptibly back and forth. He did not realise he was crying until Margaret said, almost kindly, 'Don't shame us, Thomas. Do you see your father blubbering into his soup?'

'No, of course not. I'm sorry.' Thomas wiped his eyes on his sleeve and sat forward again.

'Look, there he goes,' said Margaret Claypole suddenly. They all stood up quickly as Lord Ortellus strode off down the hall so abruptly that the herald barely had time to get the trumpet to his lips.

'And still not a word to anyone about what he means to do,' Margaret lamented.

After dinner, Thomas went upstairs to his room and threw himself down on the bed. He knew he could not stay there. His afternoon sword practice had been cancelled since the raiders came, so one of his aunts would be sure to send for him. He could not bear the thought of their company, having to read or sing for them while they sewed and whispered. He got up and stood behind the door. There was a hiding place he had used when he was little, a large chest at the bottom of the stairs. If he could get to it, he would be safe. He waited a little, then slid open his door and went quietly down the stairs. No one was in sight. Beyond the doorway that led into the hall he could hear the kitchen boys clearing the tables. He eased open the heavy lid of the chest. It was half full of lavender-scented linen. He pulled off his dirty boots and hid them out of sight behind the chest, then stepped inside, crouched down and pulled the lid over his head. It was a tight fit. He turned on to his side and drew his knees up under his chin. The smooth sheets grew warm under him and the air grew stuffy. He lay like an animal, thinking of nothing. It was not long before he fell asleep.

He woke suddenly, hearing voices. They passed very close and faded again, and Thomas then became aware of the terrible cramp in his back.

The arm he had lain on was quite numb, the fingers cold and bloated like a drowned man's. He pushed open the chest with his other hand and stepped out. He was horribly stiff, with an intense headache and thirst. He had no idea of the time. The staircase was in darkness and he could hear nothing from the hall. Shaking his numb arm back into painful life, he pulled on his boots and tugged his jacket down. He went through the doorway into the hall and began to cross it quickly. Someone – a servant – called out from the shadows, but Thomas did not stop. He reached the doorway opposite and began to climb the stairs. He did not ask himself what he was doing, or why; he simply knew he had to get to his mother's room.

Margaret Claypole did not scold him, or ask where he had been. She rose from her chair just inside the room and put her finger to her lips. Thomas looked towards the bed. A lamp had been lit and its light fell like a yellow stain on the white linen. Beside the bed knelt his father, his head level with the high pillows, holding his mother's hand. He knelt without moving, and his stillness and his silence were so strange that Thomas came forward into the light and saw his mother's wax-like face.

He turned clumsily and ran out of the room.

Moments later, Margaret Claypole followed. She came up behind him as he stared out of the window at the dark. 'I'm sorry.'

His shoulders flinched with nervous surprise as she touched him.

'We searched for you all over the castle. If you had been where you ought . . .'

'It doesn't matter,' Thomas said. His fingers prised at the cold stones of the wall. 'Was my father with her? That's all she would have cared about.'

Margaret did not attempt to deny it. 'He was there. Now go to your room. I'll come to you later. There's nothing you can do here. Care of the dead is women's business.'

Three

The afternoon following his mother's funeral, Thomas sat on the edge of his bed scraping his boots across the bare floorboards. He got up abruptly and walked around the room; reaching the table, he picked up the recorder that lay there, played a few notes and set it down again. Near his bed lay a small pack like a soldier's, with his cloak folded over it. Thomas went over and checked the straps, then glanced at the door impatiently. At last, he heard the sound of footsteps on the stairs.

'Thomas. You sent for me.' It was Margaret Claypole. She came in, shut the door, and stood with a hand on her chest, getting her breath back after the climb up the steep steps. Then she turned to Thomas, a look of enquiry on her wrinkled face.

'Have you ever seen my father trying to give an order?' Thomas burst out.

'Trying?' Margaret repeated in blank surprise.

'At the funeral,' he said impatiently. 'When the raiders broke their truce and fired arrows from the headland. My father didn't know what to do. It was the captain who sent the soldiers after them, though he made a pretence of taking his cue from Lord Ortellus. How long is this going to go on, Margaret? The raiders are burning farms within sight of the castle while our soldiers sit in the guard room because my father won't let them out to fight!'

'The raiders will never take the castle, if that's what's troubling you,' Margaret said, her eyes following him as he paced up and down.

'So we can starve while the country burns?'

'Your father won't let that happen.'

'What makes you so sure?' Thomas looked at her searchingly.

Margaret sighed. 'You're right. No one can get him to leave your mother's room. He's trying to pretend he was buried with her.'

'It's not really because of my mother, though, is it? It's because they've asked for the Sword.'

Margaret Claypole drew breath sharply, then reluctantly nodded. 'He blames himself for the loss of it. He sees all this – the raiders, your mother's death – as punishment for what happened all those years ago. He has lost all faith in himself, Thomas. If we had the Sword, your father would be out there now, beating back the raiders.'

'Exactly. That's why I'm going to get it back.'

Margaret Claypole looked at him in astonishment. 'Thomas, are you mad? You don't know what you're saying. No one knows what horrors exist in the forest, let alone the danger from Midwinter himself. And that's if you can get past the raiders outside the castle! It's quite impossible!'

Thomas smiled. 'I'm not afraid of the forest, and I'll take my chance with Midwinter,' he said. 'As for the raiders – well, I hope we can slip past them more easily than a troop of soldiers would.'

got the key to the south-west gate from the kitchen, like you told me,' Billy said.

'Good,' said Thomas, smiling back at him. 'It should be dark in an hour. We'd better get round there now. Standing here we're about as inconspicuous as a bonfire at midnight.'

It was a long wait in the cold beside the little gate. They talked eagerly at first, going over the details of the journey. Neither boy had been further than a few hours' ride from the castle, and they knew they would have to travel by night and avoid the road. After a while, though, it seemed as if nothing more could be said. They fell silent and simply waited. They were in a part of the castle that was little used and none of the familiar noises reached them. The passageway where they stood smelt of damp and rotting vegetables; the south-west gate was mainly used for throwing out rubbish, and opened on to the steepest part of the cliff, well away from the road. Outside, the ground rose steeply and there was only the roughest of tracks along the cliff. Thomas had chosen it as an unlikely place for the raiders to watch, but still, when they finished muffling the horses' hooves and Billy fished out the key, the hairs prickled on the back of Thomas's neck.

'We have to move quietly, or we've had it,' he whispered. 'Take hold of Oliver's bridle. I'll lead. If you can't see me, or want to stop, whistle quietly. And watch where you're putting your feet!'

As they began to climb, Thomas kept his mind on the plan he had worked out. The raiders held the road and the cliff opposite the castle, overlooking the harbour. It was anybody's guess where they had posted their look-outs. But there was a chance that they had left the ridge on this side of the road less well guarded. If the boys could reach the top and follow it inland, parallel to the road, eventually they would come down in farm land, miles from the castle. It was a chance. A remote one.

They climbed, feeling their way forward and encouraging the reluctant horses with whispered praise. It was impossible to move silently. The frozen earth echoed like a dull bell when struck by the horses' hooves. The harness squeaked, and every two or three paces a dislodged pebble rattled into the bushes below. The boys stumbled on the rough frozen track; once Thomas almost fell. As the dark bulk of the castle receded below them, they were exposed to the wind. Soon Thomas could no longer feel his fingers clenched round the reins and his feet stubbed the ground clumsily. The further they went the more he felt his fear growing. It became harder and harder just to keep moving.

Then suddenly he could see stars ahead. They were coming to the top of the ridge. The horses snorted gratefully and Thomas himself grinned until he felt his numbed face would crack. The ridge was empty. So far, they were safe. 'We'll go on in a bit,' he told Billy. 'Let's just rest now and keep below the skyline.'

They both turned instinctively to look down. Below them was the castle; to the left the sweep of land down to the harbour and the villages beyond. Thomas stroked his horse, Araminta, and buried his cold face in her side. Then he heard Billy's sharp intake of breath. 'My village!' Billy whispered. 'So that's where the raiders went.'

Thomas straightened up. Down below a red glow had begun to spread and suddenly flared. Thomas knew what must be happening, but he couldn't take it in. Such horror among the familiar crooked rows of cottages seemed impossible, unreal.

'What's your father doing?' Billy demanded. His voice was loud and anguished, with no thought for their discovery. 'What's he doing? Looking down from his fine castle! Or maybe he's already in bed. Maybe he's sound asleep.'

'Billy!' Thomas tried to grab him, but Billy broke away. He scrambled up to the highest point of the ridge. He started to wave his hands and shout, 'Here we are, you animals! Here's someone ready to fight! Or is it only children and old women you're after?'

Thomas stared after him, rooted with guilt, fear and pain.

No one heard him. There could be no look-outs nearby, and no shouting could reach the raiders in the village above the noise of the wind and the sea. After a while Billy came down. His face was wet and he did not look at Thomas. 'Come on,' he said tonelessly. 'Let's go.'

Thomas followed him to the horses. 'The sooner we come back with the Sword, the sooner the raiders will pay,' he said. But he didn't need to see Billy's face to know it brought no comfort. Thomas's dream of peace had never seemed so remote.

Four

They trekked along the ridge in silence for some hours. Fortunately the snow was thin on the high ground and no more fell that night. The sky began to lighten from black to deep blue and streaks of pink light appeared in the east. Suddenly Thomas halted and called back to Billy, 'It isn't safe to go on much longer. We'd better find somewhere to sleep.'

A little further on, the ridge dipped and they were able to lead the horses down into a kind of hollow from which a stream ran down to the road below. It was hard to judge how well hidden it would be in the daytime. Billy stayed with the horses while Thomas went down to the road. He moved very quietly, exploring the ground in a wide circle. By the time he came back, it was just light enough for him to see Billy waiting, a distinct black shape against the shadowy rocks and bushes.

'It looks all right,' Thomas said. 'Unless they come along the ridge right on top of us, we should be safe.'

Together they unstrapped the bedrolls from the horses and tied them securely to some bushes close to the stream. Thomas unrolled his damp bedding and wriggled between the blankets; the last sound he heard was the horses near him, drinking thirstily from the stream.

He awoke suddenly out of a confused and frightening dream. All he remembered was the end of it, when Midwinter had come up to him, the struggling bundle in his arms, and smiling horribly, had pulled back the blankets to reveal what was inside. Thomas fought to wake before he would have to see it; forced himself up into the great light of day, breathing hard. For a few minutes he just lay on his back, staring at the cold sky, glad to be out of it; then he looked around for Billy. The bed beside him was empty. Thomas sat up, and to his relief saw Billy sitting a little way downstream, wrapped in a blanket. 'When did you wake up?' he called across to him.

Billy didn't turn round. He went on staring up at the ridge. 'I haven't been asleep,' he said.

'You were supposed to wake me after the first watch,' Thomas said, annoyed. 'We were meant to be taking turns.'

Billy turned round slowly and looked at him. 'I just couldn't sleep, all right?'

Once more, Thomas felt a sense of shame. No memory of the burning village had kept him awake. 'What time is it?' he asked quickly, glancing at the grey, snow-laden clouds.

'Late morning,' Billy said. 'I had a look around. There doesn't seem to be anyone about. I think we could push on if we're careful.'

They both got to their feet. Thomas wished he hadn't. His whole body ached and his head felt thick and stupid. He hadn't had enough sleep, but he was too cold to want any more. He rolled up his blankets and walked painfully over to Araminta to strap them on her back. 'Do we get any breakfast before we start?' he called to Billy.

'If you want.'

There was only bread, and water from the stream. It did nothing to take the chill out of the morning. Though he was hungry, Thomas had to force himself to eat, and he could only swallow a few mouthfuls of the water, which was so bitterly cold it made the bones of his face ache. As they set off, leading the horses over the rocks, he lifted his eyes to try and get his bearings. The sun was hidden behind thick cloud and the compass was stowed away in his pocket, but he realised with a shock of delight that he knew, somehow, in which direction the forest lay. It was as if, without him saying a conscious word, the magic he had absorbed from the books was acting like a needle, pointing to its true north.

'Over there, where that big rock stands alone above the pine trees,' he said, smiling. 'That's the right direction, as the crow flies.'

'What are you talking about?' Billy demanded crossly.

'Never mind.' The glow inside Thomas helped him to forget the cold.

They continued along the ridge, keeping well below the skyline. This meant that the going was difficult. They had to scramble over rocks, cross streams and negotiate a thick scrub of bushes and undernourished young trees. It was so cold that a thin film of ice had formed on the sluggish water, and in many places old snow, partly thawed and then re-frozen, made the ground dangerously slippery. Thomas was nearly exhausted, but at least he knew there was little chance that the raiders would find them. The boys were hidden from the road below and they would have heard anyone coming through the bushes in plenty of time to hide.

Towards the end of the afternoon, it began to snow. Big flakes fell, thick and steady, and soon the wind rose, driving the snow in whirling shapes around them. The horses grew nervous and difficult to control; it wasn't possible to see more than a few yards ahead. Still the snow fell out of the white sky, as if the sky itself was coming down in pieces.

'This is no good,' Thomas shouted above the wind, struggling with Araminta. 'We can't go on much further, Billy.'

'Then look for some shelter. We'll freeze to death if we don't get under cover.'

Thomas blinked the snowflakes out of his eyes and peered ahead. That could be a rock, or a bush, or nothing at all. The wind swirled, and shapes danced and reformed and vanished away. Suddenly there was a noise behind him. He turned to see Billy crumple and slither down the ridge.

'Billy!' he shouted and scrambled after him.

'It's all right, I'm all right. I just slipped on some ice. I've scraped my arm, I think.' Slowly, with Thomas's help, Billy climbed back up to where the horses waited. He was crusted with snow and held his arm awkwardly. 'It'll be dark soon,' he said with a shiver that was more fear than cold. 'What are we going to do, Thomas?'

Thomas looked around him in desperation then turned to Billy. 'You stay here. I'm going on ahead.' Ignoring Billy's protests, Thomas pressed forward, with a hand in front of his face to ward off any unseen branches or jutting rocks. As soon as he thought he was out of sight, he stopped. He took a deep breath, raised his arms and began to chant. It was one of the spells he had learnt from the Chronicles, though he had never dared use it. Around him, the wind continued to howl and the snow to tumble, and Thomas could hardly hear his own voice in the storm. He began to be afraid that he had forgotten the form, or mistaken some of the words. Perhaps he was doing nothing, or even making things worse with his meddling! Then, gradually, the space between his hands began to thicken and darken, and a deep vibrating noise arose to fill it. As it grew louder the wind faltered and died away. Thomas was drawing the storm into his hands.

Thomas continued to chant and the snow began to fall more gently. Now he could see that the space between his hands was full of dark angry movement like a swarm of bees. He lifted his head. The landscape was calm and white all around him. Ahead was a large rock, its base split and the earth beneath it washed away, forming a little cave. Carefully, his hands held out before him, Thomas walked towards it and knelt down.

'Go,' he said and lowered his hands into the darkness. 'Go back under the earth and return to your rightful place.'

When he stood up, his hands were empty. He was shaking with the effort of concentration, wet with sweat, but filled with elation.

'Thomas!' Behind him Billy was calling. 'Thomas, up there! It's stopped snowing. I can see a hut at the top of the ridge!'

Once they were safely inside the hut, Billy wrapped himself in his blankets and fell asleep almost at once. Thomas could not sleep. He felt unsettled and restless; his mind raced from topic to topic uncontrollably. He thought about the spell he had just cast and then about Midwinter and the forest. Billy groaned in his sleep and Thomas watched him for a while, remembering the attack on the village. He had met Billy's father and his sister; he tried to imagine what Billy was feeling, not knowing if they were alive. He wished Billy would share his thoughts. He wished he knew what he could do to help.

Outside, the sky gradually darkened and night fell. Thomas let his thoughts slide away from Billy. He was longing for a fire and hot food and dry clothes. His imagination so warmed to them that he could almost feel the heat of a blaze on his chilled face and chest. It was torture to open his eyes and see only the cold cramped hut. He was very hungry. In Billy's pack, he knew, there was only oatmeal and a little saltfish and some bread, nothing anyone would want to eat. Desperate to turn his thoughts to something else, he got up and went to the door of the hut and looked out. It was a clear night. The moon was high and full and the stars glittered coldly above the milk-white hill. The rocks and the bushes were blurred and blunted with snow. Nothing was moving. Thomas felt the profound stillness touch him as his eyes swept over the silent hillside. Then suddenly, down below him, where the road curved round the base of the hill, he saw a flicker of light. It had to be a camp fire. He tried to guess the distance, but his heart was banging so wildly it was hard for him to think. If raiders were down there, they were so close a well aimed stone would hit them! He turned and looked at Billy, still sleeping at the back of the hut.

'Billy!' he called out softly.

Billy stirred and muttered, but did not wake up.

Thomas knew what he ought to do. He ought to shake Billy awake, get the horses and make a dash for it. Instead he crept quietly out of the hut and down the hill.

The moonlight reflected off the snow, making it easy for Thomas to find his way. The spark of the campfire flickered through the bushes down below, now to his right, now to his left. Then suddenly it disappeared. Thomas halted, realising it must mean he was getting close to the raiders. Only then did he grasp the danger of his situation and begin to be afraid. It was darker here than on the slope of the hill and he could stumble into the raiders' camp without even knowing it. There were thick bushes on either side of him; ahead through a narrow gap he could just see the snow dip steeply as it covered the road. Suddenly a low voice growled in Thomas's ear. 'We should have stayed in that barn, not set off across country in a mad race to catch up with the others.'

Thomas nearly screamed aloud in shock. He squatted down where he stood, his heart pounding as though he had just run a race.

'You were the one who said it wouldn't snow, Stefan.' This voice was milder, but still held the lilting accent of the Dalmatic Islanders.

Thomas peered through the bushes. He could see the fire just ahead and three or four shadowy figures around it. He had nearly walked straight into them! He hardly dared breathe now, terrified he would make a sound and give himself away.

'I hate this country.' That was Stefan again. 'All it's good for is a few skinny cows and sheep. I don't know why anyone would want it, let alone why we had to invade it at this miserable time of year.'

'You know why we came, so stop complaining.' It was a third speaker, who sounded older than the others. 'We haven't come for spoils. We've come to take back what was ours in the days before the wars.'

'When the Sword is Erik's, the islands will recognise one Lord again and the feuding will be over,' the mild voice put in. 'Surely that's worth a little misery?'

'We are Erik's men,' said the stern one. 'We have to follow him, however strange the adventure. And if he does succeed no one need come raiding here again.'

'Maybe, if the Rossendale butchers leave us be,' Stefan said sourly. 'In the meantime, Erik's snug in a ship in the castle harbour, and we're here in the snow.'

'Well, you're better off than poor Martin,' the mild voice was beginning, when Thomas felt an irresistible tickle in his nose. He did what he could – pinched his nose between his fingers, and held his breath – but the sneeze, when it came, was a huge explosion. He did not wait for the raiders to finish shouting and grab their weapons, he just ran. He plunged through the bushes, not caring about noise or tracks, but he did not make straight for the hut. He had just enough presence of mind to zigzag along the bottom of the hill until, lungs bursting, he leapt a frozen ditch and flattened himself among the bushes on the other side.

He heard the raiders coming towards him.

'Forget it, Stefan,' one shouted. 'Whoever it was, we scared them off.'

'Probably just some farm-boy,' said the other, and laughed. 'He thought he was a hero till he saw our swords.'

But Stefan's boots thudded across the ditch. 'He came through here. You can see the snow's all trampled.'

Thomas hugged the ground, scarcely breathing. A moment later a sword stabbed through the bushes inches above his head. His mind searched for a spell that would help him, and he began to murmur the words of a shielding chant. The sword jabbed through the bushes again, straight into Thomas's face. But it was Stefan who let out a yell of pain and dropped his weapon.

'I jarred my arm,' he complained. 'That bush must be frozen as hard as iron.'

'Leave it, Stefan! You'll never find him,' the mild one protested.

'I'm going back.' That was the older one. 'I want to eat.'

Stefan growled something indistinguishable. Then slowly the footsteps receded. But it was a long time before Thomas got up and made his way back to the hut.

To his dismay, Billy was standing in the doorway of the hut looking out over the hill. When he saw Thomas, he didn't need to speak. His expression said everything.

'Sorry,' Thomas said, wretchedly bringing out the lie he had prepared. 'While you were asleep, I saw a rabbit and chased it down the hill. I thought we could cook it, only I lost track of it and then I got lost, and . . .'

'Rubbish!' Billy interrupted angrily. 'What sort of fool do you think I am, Thomas? There's a fire down at the bottom of the hill. You went after them, didn't you?'

Thomas slid past him into the hut. 'If we're going to argue, at least let's do it inside,' he said.

'Argue!' Billy grabbed him by the shoulder and pulled him round to face him. 'Beat your silly brains out, more like. I thought they'd killed you, Thomas. You were gone so long, I thought you must be dead.' Thomas stared at him, guilty and surprised. Billy went on, 'You left your footprints in the snow all the way down the hill. A blind man could track his way back up here! I thought you were them, coming after me. I didn't know whether to stay and fight, or whether it was my job to go on to the forest alone.'

'Billy . . .' Thomas put his hand out to touch his friend's arm, but Billy shrugged it off.

'Forget it,' he said. 'It was such a stupid thing to do, that's all.'

'I know.' Thomas gazed at Billy, then looked down the hill. Once more he saw how close the camp was, and thought with horror of what he could have done to Billy. 'I just didn't think. When I saw them down there, I just wanted to *do* something, you know the feeling?'

Billy nodded. 'And you thought you could get away with doing it on your own before I woke up,' he said with a faint grin. 'They didn't give you any trouble, then?'

Thomas hesitated. 'No,' he lied. 'They didn't even see me.'

Billy smiled with a savage pleasure Thomas did not understand.

'All the same, we'd better get moving,' Billy said. 'We'll lead the horses down to the road and then ride. Unless we run into a whole gang of them camping on the road itself, we should be all right. They may see us, but they won't have horses to follow.'

'If you think it's worth the risk,' Thomas said doubtfully.

'Time's getting on. What do you think is happening at the castle now?'

It was impossible to answer. In silence, the two boys made ready and set off.

They rode between snowy moonlit fields until dawn, encountering no one. The horses grew tired, and the boys let them trot and then walk, themselves too tired to speak. As the sun rose, Thomas started to have trouble keeping his eyes open. A bird was singing somewhere, a high monotonous thread of sound that grew smaller and smaller as the comfortable darkness in his head flowed out to fill the road. Then he felt a rough shove in his ribs and opened his eyes with a jerk.

'You were nearly off then,' Billy said.

'Sorry.' Thomas blinked hard and tried to force his eyes wide open. The road was filled with floating red and black specks, and he couldn't seem to shake them away. 'I need to sleep,' he admitted in surprise.

'Soon,' said Billy. 'We'll find somewhere off the road.'

A short time later he pointed over the hedge. 'What about over there?'

Thomas looked. It was a farm, with a long low house and a taller barn forming two sides of the yard. A track led from the road up to the house. Across another field were some outbuildings and a cottage. It took Thomas some time to realise what was wrong. The snow was undisturbed by any sign of movement. The yard was empty and silent. There wasn't even any smoke coming from the farmhouse chimney.

'Something's happened. I don't like it, Billy. I think we should go on. It isn't safe.'

'Sneaking down to the raiders' camp wasn't safe. If the raiders came here they left before the snow.'

'Or they're still inside,' Thomas said.

But Billy was already riding ahead. He turned down the track to the farm without looking back to see if Thomas would follow. Thomas let him get almost half-way down before he touched Araminta into motion and set off after him. He was angry, but as much with himself as with Billy. If he hadn't gone off without Billy the night before, Billy wouldn't be taking risks in broad daylight now. But whatever there was to face, they would have to face it together. He caught up with Billy and they rode into the farmyard side by side.

'Any raiders at home?' Billy called in a low facetious voice that made Thomas wince. No one replied. They waited a long moment, then Billy swung down from his horse and went over to the house. The door was standing open and the door frame and lintel were blackened as though someone had tried to start a fire. Something greyish-white was lying across the doorway. It took Thomas a moment to realise it was a naked arm. Billy stooped down and touched the dead fingers. Then he went inside the house. He came out quickly, looking white and shaken.

'Don't go in. You can guess. There's no need to see.' Billy went over to the water-butt in the yard, broke the ice with his fist and looked at the water. He could not drink.

'It must have been the raiders I saw last night,' Thomas said. 'I heard them talking. They said something about a barn.'

'They must have driven off all the animals,' Billy said. 'They'll have taken only a few chickens or geese; whatever they could kill and carry easily. The farmer would have given them those at the sight of a sword. No need for . . .' He pushed himself upright abruptly, took a few steps away and bent forward to be sick. Thomas watched him unhappily. Behind Billy, he could see the door of the house out of the corner of his eye. He didn't want to know and yet he did. 'Let's go,' he urged Billy. 'We can find somewhere else to sleep, somewhere clean and safe.'

Billy straightened up and looked at him. 'There's no hurry, is there?' He walked towards the barn. He pulled open the door and went inside. After a moment Thomas heard him give a low whistle. Then Billy came running out, his face full of savage joy. 'Come and have a look,' he said. 'There's one of them in there.'

He took Thomas by the arm and pulled him towards the barn. When they got inside Thomas could see nothing at first. Light leaked in through the gaps in the plank walls. The air was full of straw dust, making him cough.

'Over here,' Billy called. He beckoned him to the furthest corner of the barn, where there was a manger and a broken milking-stool. Lying between them, as if for shelter, was a man. Thomas thought he was dead at first, for his eyes were closed and his jacket was clogged and black with dried blood. Then he snorted and moved his head restlessly, and the boy saw that water and a loaf had been placed within his reach.

'They couldn't take him along,' said Billy. 'So they left him here.'

He was a small man with a straggling red beard and a badly-scarred face. He looked surprisingly old. His breathing was laboured, and he seemed unaware of them bending over him.

'The farm-boys fought back, didn't they?' Billy's voice was jubilant. 'You didn't expect that.' He nudged the raider in the ribs with the toe of his boot, making him groan.

'Don't,' said Thomas. 'He's dying.'

'I can see that. Tell you what, I'll finish the business for him.' Billy looked round the barn. There was a hay fork hanging on the wall. He took it down and swung it from hand to hand. 'Once through the throat. That'd do it.'

Thomas turned to face him. 'Billy, he's dying anyway,' he said urgently. 'Leave him alone.'

Billy continued to pass the fork from hand to hand, an expression of greedy excitement on his face. Thomas was suddenly very afraid. He stood between Billy and the raider. 'It's wrong,' he said.

'You had your fun last night,' Billy said fiercely. 'It's my turn now.'

Thomas groaned. 'Billy, you misunderstood me. I didn't kill anyone.'

Billy stared at him. 'Then what did you do?'

'I just wanted to spy on them. I just wanted to see what they were like, hear them talk.'

'And did you? Did you hear them talk about what they did to the people here? And you just turned round and left them to their talk?'

'No!' Thomas was shouting now. 'It wasn't like that! And if I had heard them talking about this, I don't know whether I would have tried to kill them. Billy, I heard something important, something I wouldn't have heard if I'd just charged in with a knife like you. They don't want to fight us, and they don't want to stay here. They just want the Sword. They say it used to belong to them. If they get it back, they won't come here again.'

Billy looked at him with contempt and anger. He let the fork slide down on to the ground. 'You're as mad as Midwinter,' he said, and turned and walked out of the barn.

Thomas stared after him for a while, then went to try and give the dying man some water.

When Thomas left the barn he saw to his relief that Billy was waiting for him in the farmyard. 'I wasn't sure you'd still be here,' he said with a tentative smile.

Billy shook his head. 'Where you go, I go, you know that. I shouldn't have said what I did.'

Thomas turned and scanned the fields for signs of movement. 'We should leave now. They could return for him.'

Billy looked mutinous. 'We stay. We need to sleep remember. And I hope they do come. You know why I want to kill the lot of them.'

'Our village.'

Billy nodded.

'Your family's bound to be all right,' Thomas said hesitantly. 'Your father's a resourceful man, quick-thinking. He'll have got them all out before the fire took hold.'

Billy lifted his shoulders as if settling them under a burden. 'Well, the sooner we get back with the Sword, the sooner we'll know,' he said.

They made camp in one of the outhouses. Billy lay down and slept almost at once, but Thomas, although tired, was too uneasy to sleep for a long time. When it was dark they ate and went on their way. Outside, the air was warmer and the snow was soft and watery underfoot.

'The thaw's started,' Billy said.

They passed the barn on their way back to the road. Thomas, who had visited the dying raider while Billy was still asleep, kept his eyes carefully averted.

'You wouldn't have killed him even if he'd been able to fight,' Billy said suddenly.

'Yes, I would,' Thomas said. But he remembered the raider's face, his scars and his thin beard. It was hard to think of killing someone when you could see their face.

'How can you be an Ortellus and not like fighting?' Billy persisted.

'There are other ways of fighting than with swords and fire. How long have the raids gone on, Billy? And what good have they ever done?'

They rode on in silence. For some reason Thomas thought of his mother for the first time since leaving the castle. Now, to his dismay, he found he couldn't quite picture her face. Dark hair and dark eyes, he told himself. And he remembered quite distinctly the pattern of her dress.

'I think I'd rather die than kill someone,' he said.

Billy twisted round in his saddle and stared at him, angry again. 'Dying yourself is easy. You lie down and die if you want. But the rest of us are going to fight for those who cannot, and we're going to win!'

Five

By morning the snow had gone and the muddy green of the fields spread wide and flat beyond the hawthorn hedges. Sheep were grazing undisturbed but the shepherds' huts were deserted. They passed through a tiny village of shuttered houses where only the dogs gave chase, barking excitedly.

'Why are they all hiding?' Billy asked impatiently. 'The raiders won't come this far west. Not when their aim is the castle.'

'Perhaps the raiders forgot to tell them that,' Thomas retorted.

'Very funny,' Billy said in a sarcastic tone.

They had been bickering ever since they left the farm, the tension of their unresolved quarrel emerging every time they spoke.

'Let's get a few hours' sleep,' Thomas suggested. 'The next hut we come to . . .'

'Fine,' Billy agreed. 'If you're not afraid of raiders jumping out at us.'

Thomas bit back an angry reply. 'There's one just by that gate.' He pointed down the road and then urged Araminta into a canter so he wouldn't have to stay at Billy's side.

They slept, ate, and went on their way in the late afternoon. Ahead of them the fields were smaller and irregularly shaped, climbing the sides of a series of rounded hills. From the top of each they could see for miles, the scattered little farms and settlements and the hard white line of the coast. One hill ahead of them was bigger than all the rest. At dusk Thomas nodded towards it.

'See that, Billy? The forest lies just beyond that hill.'

'How can you be sure?' Billy demanded. 'Neither of us have ever been this far west.'

Thomas smiled. 'I just know. We must ride through the night. We'll be there by the morning.'

But it took longer than Thomas expected to reach the great hill. It was already dawn when they began to climb. As they toiled up, murmuring encouragement to the tired horses, the sun rose behind them. Cold winter sunshine filled the sky and lit up the landscape of rocks and moor. When at last they reached the top, Thomas dismounted and ran forward to stare down into the forest. It was even more impressive and fearful than he had imagined, stretching like a black cloak over the land further than he could see. Billy came up behind him. Uneasily, he muttered, 'The road just ends. It's swallowed up by trees.'

'What else did you expect?'

'I don't know,' Billy said. 'I didn't really expect to get this far.'

'Come on.' Thomas turned to him in excitement. 'We can ride straight down.' He ran back to the horses, hardly noticing how slowly Billy followed.

They were almost at the bottom of the hill, when Billy said, 'Stop a bit. I want a drink.' Thomas waited impatiently as Billy got down, drank and slowly replaced the bottle in his saddle-bag.

'What did Midwinter come here for?' Billy asked. 'It feels like the end of the world.'

'For the adventure, maybe,' Thomas replied. 'Even without the Sword he might have come here to learn magic.'

'From the green people?' Billy had tried to make a joke of it, but when Thomas nodded, his scorn was profound. 'Midwinter just needed a place to hide where no one would come after him. It'll take us years to find him in the forest, if he's not already dead. The Sword's gone, Thomas. I don't think your father meant us to find it at all.'

Thomas looked at him, and decided not to reply.

They rode on, no longer talking. Soon there were trees crowding on either side of them. The light fell through an arch of branches and the road was thick with leaf mould. Thomas felt a tingling in his nerves as the trees enclosed them, a sensation of recognition. He had entered the place of the old stories, the place of magic. He turned to Billy in delight, and got a shock. Billy's face was a mask of fear, white and drawn. He met Thomas's stare with a snarl. 'Don't look at me like that! What's the matter with you?'

'You're frightened,' Thomas said in wonder.

'Of course I'm frightened,' Billy snapped. 'So would you be if you weren't the biggest fool in Rossendale.'

That only made Thomas want to laugh. 'This isn't Rossendale,' he said.

Billy's eyes shifted from Thomas to the trees beyond. 'I know it isn't,' he said.

They went on in silence for a little while. Billy kept swinging round in his saddle to look through the trees behind them.

'What is it?' Thomas asked. 'What can you see?'

Billy didn't answer. But a little later he halted and started to speak in a low fast gabble. 'If we lose the road we'll never get back. We'll wander here till we die. And there are things all around us, Thomas, things watching – I can sense it.'

'So can I,' Thomas said gently. 'But they're nothing to be afraid of.'

Billy lifted his head and stared at him. 'I wanted to die at home, fighting the raiders. Not here, where we don't belong. I don't believe your father sent us here to get the Sword. He sent us here to get rid of you.'

Thomas was too shocked to speak for a moment. Then he said quietly and clearly, 'No one sent us here to die, Billy. You're frightened and you're not thinking straight.'

Billy laughed. 'I'm thinking straight for the first time. It's what the others at the castle have always said about you, though I could never see it. Only when I saw you gazing down at the forest with that smile on your face, did I realise. It's what your father could never stand, why he sent us here. You're like *him* aren't you? You're the same as Midwinter.'

Thomas was angry now, angry and deeply hurt. He got down off Araminta and unstrapped his pack.

'What are you doing?' Billy demanded.

Thomas swung his pack on to his shoulders. 'I can manage without you. Go home. I'm going on alone.'

Billy dismounted. Even as he walked towards Thomas, he couldn't help glancing round uneasily at the trees. 'I can't leave you. I have to stay.'

'Because my father said so?' Thomas asked coldly. 'Even though he sent us here to die?'

Billy nodded miserably. 'It must be true. He doesn't love you. Everyone knows it. He tries, but he can't. He hasn't been able to love you since Philip died.'

'Who's Philip?' Thomas asked. When Billy didn't answer, he shouted it. 'Who is Philip?'

'I don't know exactly,' Billy admitted, shaken. 'Your brother, maybe. The servants stop talking when they see I'm near. But he disappeared the same time as Midwinter. I think Midwinter killed him.'

Thomas looked down and saw a stone. He picked it up. 'Go away, Billy,' he said.

'Just because I'm telling you the truth?' Billy shouted.

Thomas threw the stone at him and hit him on the shin. He bent down to pick up another.

'Thomas, don't be stupid!' Billy protested, rubbing his leg.

Thomas threw the second stone, hitting Billy on the shoulder. Billy gave a shout of pain and walked forward with his hands raised to protect his face. Thomas drew his knife. 'Go home,' he said. 'I don't want you with me.'

Billy answered in a dogged voice, desperate beyond fear, 'Your father sent me. I have to stay.'

Thomas laughed spitefully. 'My father didn't send us here. So what does that do for your precious theory? The whole idea was mine, and my father knows nothing about it. I only told you he did to make you come.' And without looking to see Billy's response, he turned and ran into the trees.

Six

By the time Thomas had calmed down enough to stop and look behind him, he saw to his dismay that it was already too late to find his way back. He had been following a path through the trees, or so he thought. Now it was as if the trees had closed behind him, leaving no trace of the path behind. He waited for a while, hoping Billy would appear. When nothing happened, he took a random plunge through the trees, trying to hit upon the path. None of it looked familiar. Had that fallen trunk, that huge formation of fungi been there as he had rushed by angrily? He had a horrible sense of the forest shifting behind his back as he walked, but he pushed the idea away quickly. He shouted, 'Billy! Billy! I'm over here!' There was no answering cry. The deep silence of the forest pressed in on him, and for the first time, he felt a little afraid. 'Let him go then, the coward,' he said unfairly. 'I'll be better off on my own.'

He set off through the dark pine trees, growing more optimistic as he walked. In all the stories he had read, the green people appeared almost as soon as the young prince set his foot in the forest. The sensation he had of being watched was very strong. Above the noise of the wind he heard snatches of laughter and voices and once, he turned quickly to catch a flash of bright green in the depths of the trees behind him. But as time went on, he began to grow puzzled and angry. If the green people knew he was here, why didn't they show themselves, speak to him, and let him ask for their help? He felt as if they were playing with him, teasing him like a clumsy animal who lacked their quickness and skill. He had no magic to force them to come out, but the urgency of his quest made him impatient. He could not afford to spend days wandering through the forest till he found a sign to lead him to Midwinter.

Occupied in his thoughts, he gave less heed to where he was going. Suddenly he found himself on the edge of a clearing. The trees all around it were stunted, their leaves a sickly yellow. There was no ground cover, and the bare brown earth was parched and cracked. In the middle of the clearing grew a short bulbous tree, whose trunk rose out of the dry earth, swollen with sap. Its thick green branches waved sinuously, as if in a current of water. There was something horrible about the luxuriant growth of that tree, when everything around it was dead or dying. Thomas, against his will, found himself drawn forward. He noticed there were red markings all the way up the trunk of the tree, like a sprinkling of blood. The branches began to undulate more quickly, moving towards Thomas as he approached. Without warning, a strong green tentacle whipped out and curled round his chest.

Thomas cried out and struggled, but the grip around him was tightening, crushing him, making it impossible to breathe. He was lifted off his feet and drawn in towards the trunk. He could smell its bitter digestive sap as he fought for life. He could no longer see, no longer think; he heard some commotion, a confusion of shouting voices, something whizzing through the air. Suddenly the intolerable pressure slackened and released. He fell down on to the ground, gasping. A voice in his ear murmured, 'Go carefully through the forest, stranger. It is a place of danger as well as delight.'

When Thomas raised his head, he saw the severed branch that had held him, still writhing on the ground beside him. But the green people who had saved him had disappeared as quickly as they'd arrived.

As soon as he was able, Thomas forced himself to go on. He wanted to get as far away from that evil place as he could. He walked until he reached a little glade with a stream running through it. There he sat down to rest, drinking and refilling his water bottle. As he looked round he realised it was getting darker. The sun was going down beyond the trees and it would soon be night. He wished that Billy was with him. He wondered where he was or even if he were alive.

He felt vulnerable and afraid. Already, in the deep shadows anything could be moving. Could the green people protect him from what stirred in the forest at night? He needed a fire, to have light and warmth close by. He got up and began to gather fallen branches from under the trees around the clearing. The timber was fairly dry and he laid it carefully with plenty of dry bracken to receive the spark from the tinder box. Then he kicked at the stupid thing with a cry of frustration. The tinder box was in Billy's pack. He had nothing with which to light the fire.

Sitting down again, Thomas thought hard. He knew of a spell that might work, but as he was gathering his powers to use it, the air was filled suddenly with the noise of wings. From across the glade came the shriek of a hunted mouse. There was a cry of pain; then silence. Thomas shivered. He realised that to use magic in the forest would attract attention more surely even than firelight. He decided to sit quietly, and endure the cold and the fear, until morning brought new light and new counsel. Night fell, and the damp air wrapped around him like a sheet. The noise of the stream grew louder. He began to hear other noises, strange chattering high up in the trees, and screeches of malicious laughter. He told himself that it was the wind. But the lights flickering in the tops of the trees were not the wind. The hissing and snuffling near his feet was not the wind. Not all the stories in the Chronicles had ended happily, he remembered. He understood Billy's fear now. It was his own.

In the darkness of the glade a milk-white shape appeared. Thomas stared at it in uncertainty. He told himself it was mist moving over the ground. As it came closer, he tried to make out its shape. A moaning sound floated across the clearing, bringing him to his feet. Whatever it was, he preferred to go forward than wait for it to come to him. On legs as stiff as stilts he crossed the dark ground, his mouth too dry for speech.

In another moment he laughed aloud in pure relief. He could see now it was a white doe, trembling at the edge of the trees in fear of him. To his surprise she did not turn and run as he approached. Tentatively he held out his fingers for her to sniff. The doe snuffled and plunged her muzzle into his curved palm; he stretched his other arm along her neck and began stroking the warm short-napped hide where her shoulder blades delicately jutted up. After a minute he led her forward into the clearing. The doe followed him, limping heavily. Thomas stopped and, bending down, felt a sticky trail of blood on the animal's left foreleg.

With one hand still stroking the doe's neck, he tried to trace the extent of the wound. The doe struggled free of him, and leapt away. She stood at a distance, trembling and fixed.

'I'm sorry,' Thomas said, feeling foolish. 'I was only trying to help.'

The doe went on watching him; she didn't move. Thomas turned and found his pack, almost stumbling over it in the dark. 'Look,' he said. 'I've got a shirt in here. If you'll only let me help you, I can tear it up and use it for a bandage.'

When he approached with the long strips of cloth in his hand, the doe stood quietly. And though he felt her tremble as he touched the upper part of the wounded leg, she did not move away. There was just enough light from the sliver of moon above the trees to make out a jagged tear in the doe's flesh. Thomas poured some water from his water bottle over the first strip and made it into a wad to press over the wound. Then he bound it in place with the other strips. It made a clumsy and inadequate dressing, but nevertheless he was pleased to have done it. When he had finished, the doe suddenly dropped her head and nuzzled his side.

'Do you want to stay with me?' Thomas asked.

The doe returned his stare gravely.

Thomas laughed and went to find his pack. As he unrolled his blankets and lay down he felt a new lightness of heart. He could sleep without fear now. The doe, he knew, would wake him at any sign of danger and tomorrow . . . Thomas curled his arm round his head and went to sleep.

He woke reluctantly, dragged out of his dreams by an insistent pain in the shoulder. He rolled on to his side and then his back, staring up at the dark green firs that rose on the bank above the stream. The light was strong, the sky overhead patched with blue. Thomas lay quietly, trying to remember what he had dreamt about.

'Who's Philip?'

The voice so echoed his thoughts that Thomas answered without thinking. 'I don't know. Billy was only guessing when he said he was my brother.' Then his heart jumped, and he sat up in a hurry. A girl of about his own age stood at his feet. A badly-tied bandage was slipping down her left arm. She was of slight build, naked, and her skin and hair were as green as grass.

'You were talking in your sleep,' she said. 'I thought you would never wake up. It's been light for hours.'

Thomas scrambled to his feet and stared at her. She stared back. Her eyes were the colour of a new leaf and the hairs of her eyebrows sprang up like tiny green shoots.

'Were you the doe last night?' he asked, trying not to sound as amazed as he felt.

She nodded. 'They were hunting me as a deer.' She touched her arm gingerly. 'This was done by a hunter of another clan. He did not know me.'

She walked past him suddenly and knelt down by the stream. She began to lap the water with her mouth, then, as if remembering, brought her hands together with a jerk and used them as a cup. When she had finished she stood up again, shaking the water from her fingers and sucking them to warm them.

'My name is Luka. It means swift runner. A long time ago, before I could walk in the forest alone, I went with my mother to pick mushrooms. Suddenly two men like you, from the naked country, came crashing through the trees. My mother pulled me away to hide, but I was young and full of curiosity. I had heard that outsiders were white as clouds. I wanted to see that. I broke free from my mother's hand and ran after the strangers, not caring where I was going.

'But the forest is full of danger if you are young or ignorant. There are places where the unseen ones gather, and places full of evil from long ago. Running into a glade, I lost sight of the strangers and knew I had entered a perilous place. Before I could turn back, I felt a pain in my backbone as though it was growing out of my skin. My arms stretched down to the ground and as my fingers touched the earth they weren't fingers any more. The forest changed around me; the smell of my mother, among all the other scents and smells, as she came seeking me, sent me running away through the trees.

'As I ran out of the glade I passed the outsiders. One of them, the tall one, called after me and held out his hand. My terror left me and I turned back and approached him. He had the bearing of a chief though his clothes were dirty and plain. There was pity in his voice as he spoke. "I cannot lift the curse on you, but I can reshape it," he said. "You will keep this form until someone of my blood comes hunting in the forest. All I ask is that when you are free again, you will help him in his hunt." '

'Midwinter!' Thomas said. 'It must have been Midwinter! Then he knew that I would come!' He turned to the green girl who was watching him. 'Luka, I came into the forest to find the man who spoke to you. Will you help me look for him?'

Luka smiled. 'I will take you to him, but it's a long day's walking. First we need to eat, and . . .' she hesitated for a moment. 'Do you have anything I could put on?'

'Of course.' Thomas dug into his pack to pull out his torn shirt. 'One sleeve's gone on this, but I've some leggings as well, and you could have a blanket for a cloak.'

Once dressed in his familiar clothes, Luka looked even more alien. Thomas was glad when she smiled, tugging at the folds of her improvised cloak. 'It all feels rather heavy, but it's warm. Thank you.'

'And I have food,' Thomas said. 'Nothing much, just some bread and dried fish. We could have made porridge, but there isn't a fire.'

Luka stared at him, wrinkling her nose. 'You don't know how to make fire?'

'Of course I do, only I don't have a tinderbox and last night I didn't like to use a spell.'

Luka nodded. 'That was wise. The unseen ones were busy in the place where I found you.'

'Unseen ones?'

'Creatures of the forest like us. But they can be malicious if disturbed. By daylight we should be safe enough. I'll make a fire, and then you can explain about the tinderbox.'

They ate hungrily, and when the meal was over sat in silence, watching the flames of the small fire. Thomas felt shy and strange, and he was glad when Luka finally spoke.

'Why are you seeking the magician? You know my story and my name, but I don't know yours.'

'True enough.' Thomas met her calm green gaze with some pride. 'My name is Thomas Ortellus. My father is Lord of Rossendale and Midwinter, your magician, is my uncle. He stole something that was not his to take, something we now need desperately. I've come to get it back.'

Luka's expression hardened. 'The magician is not a thief. He has not broken a twig of the forest that he did not need. You people of the outside, you are the ones that waste and steal. We have heard about your wars and your killing. When you are a man, will you lead the killing, Thomas Ortellus?'

Thomas did not answer that. He said defensively, 'We don't just fight. There are farmers growing food, and people making things, and people studying. The fighting is only because we have to, because the raiders come.'

Luka was not convinced. 'Perhaps it started as necessity, but I think your people enjoy killing. Hunters used to come here from outside before they grew too afraid. They would leave three or four slaughtered deer behind them and carry one away. And if a forester challenged them, they would leave his carcass too.'

Thomas was ashamed. 'I didn't know that. I thought in the old days people came here to learn about the forest.'

'At the beginning,' Luka agreed. 'Then they thought they knew.'

Thomas got to his feet. 'Your magician sounds too good to be the Midwinter I know,' he said.

'Unless your story is a lie.'

Thomas shook his head impatiently. 'It's the truth, Luka. Please, don't you think it's time we made a start? You said it was a day's journey.'

Luka jumped up. 'If we walk quickly we might reach the lake by nightfall.'

'Lake?' Thomas said in surprise.

'The magician lives on an island in the middle of the lake. I can take you to the lakeside. After that . . .'

Thomas pulled a wry face. 'After that I have a long cold swim. Well, let's pack up the things and start walking.'

They took it in turns to carry the pack, but even when Luka had it she ran ahead of Thomas on silent feet. Thomas guessed she was angry with him and he was too proud himself to ask her to slow down. Sometimes he lost sight of her among the trees but always, just as he was beginning to lose his nerve, he would glimpse her ahead, a flash of bright colour against the dark green. Other times she waited for him to catch up, but was off again with a glance and a laugh as soon as he reached her.

It was a cold day and it grew colder as the sun dipped below the tops of the trees, but Thomas was sweating as he hurried after Luka. At last he came to a clearing made by the fall of a well-grown beech tree that lay covered in brambles, its huge roots twisted out of the earth. Luka was squatting down on her heels with her back to the fallen tree. As Thomas came up she patted the ground beside her. Grateful for the rest, though still angry, he sat down at her side.

'I am sorry. You are not used to the forest. I should not have gone so fast. But it has been strange for me too, using my eyes now, and losing the smells and the sounds. I suppose I wanted to find out if I could still find my way.'

'And to punish me for saying what I know about Midwinter,' Thomas put in crossly.

Luka had the grace to look a little ashamed. 'You are of his family, but he has lived among the forest people for years. He has done nothing but good here.'

Thomas decided not to renew the argument. Instead he asked, 'What about your family, Luka? How soon will you see them again?' He wondered as he spoke how she must feel, delaying the joy and surprise of her homecoming for the sake of a quest that was not hers.

Luka looked at the ground for a moment before replying. 'They did not come near me all the time I was under the spell. They were too afraid. At first it was hard, but now I am used to being alone. My mother is dead now, and my brothers are grown up and have children of their own. I do not know if I want to go back, Thomas. It has been too long a time.'

'But you should at least let them see you. You should tell them what has happened.'

Luka looked at him in bewilderment. Then her face cleared. 'You are an outsider,' she remembered. 'My clan know what has happened. They have been watching since we left this morning. One or two are watching now.'

Thomas followed her glance towards the surrounding trees. He could see nothing, but he did not doubt Luka's word.

'I will take you to Midwinter,' she said firmly. 'Then I will know what to do.'

They walked on after a rest and a drink of cold water. It was Thomas's turn to carry the pack, but Luka did not hand it over. With Billy he might have felt resentful, but it wasn't possible to get into competition with Luka. She walked more slowly now, and he kept close behind her, trying to ignore the aches in his back and legs. It was growing colder and darker, but Luka seemed to know her way through the trees even without the light. She would warn Thomas of low branches and other hazards, stopping to take his arm and guide him if it was needed. Night closed around them and still they continued. Thomas stretched out one hand to touch Luka's shoulder and they went even more slowly. The noises of the night no longer alarmed Thomas, but they prompted him to ask Luka something.

'Luka, your people tracked me through the forest. They came to help me when I was in danger, but they didn't stay to ask me why I was here. Why was that?'

Luka laughed. 'No one would willingly approach an outsider. We know you are easily alarmed and use your weapons quickly. But no one would want you to get into danger either. You did not know your way through the forest. You might easily have come to harm as I did in the dark places.'

Thomas shivered, remembering the tree. 'But Midwinter found his way,' he said.

'Midwinter is a magician. He knew how to protect himself and those with him.'

'Those with him?' Thomas echoed uneasily.

'There was another man, with a simple face and a limp. And didn't I tell you? Midwinter was carrying a young child.'

Thomas was too stunned to speak. The image of Midwinter with a struggling bundle in his arms returned to him in all its familiar horror.

'Listen,' said Luka. 'Can you hear the stream? When we reach it, the path will be easier.' She began to walk on and Thomas followed her like a blind man, his mind full of doubt and foreboding.

Seven

Even before they reached the lake, Thomas sensed it was ahead of them. A breeze began, bringing with it a muddy freshwater smell. Behind the noisy rush of the stream he thought he could hear a deeper sound of waves lapping, and the ground began to slope a little. Then suddenly there was nothing ahead of them, the trees parted and, black against a paler sky, the lake appeared. Thomas walked forward and the soil under his feet crunched faintly, as if it was mixed with sand.

'Don't go too close,' Luka cautioned. 'You don't want to leave the shelter of the trees.'

'But I can see something. What is that, a light?'

It was out in the middle of the water, a tiny spark. 'It's the magician's fire,' Luka whispered. 'He keeps it burning all night.'

Thomas watched it for a while. He wondered if Midwinter was awake, sitting by the flame.

'Come on,' said Luka. 'We should make our own fire. We need to eat and then sleep.'

Thomas gave her what help he could. When the fire was lit and the porridge cooking, he said, 'I wish there was another way to get across to the island. I don't really want to meet Midwinter when I'm soaking wet and shivering.'

'Wait and see what happens,' said Luka, coming to sit beside him. 'My clan weren't the only ones tracking us through the woods.'

Thomas turned to her uneasily. 'What do you mean?'

But Luka wouldn't say any more. 'Wait until tomorrow. They can see our fire, just as we can see theirs.'

When Thomas woke, Luka was moving beside him. The fire was out and it was day. He could see the island across the grey water. Like the surrounding land it was covered in trees, with a narrow strip of sandy soil coming down to the water's edge. There was no one on the shore. It was only as Thomas turned his head to look along the curve of the lake that he noticed a boat in the water, coming from the island.

'Luka!' he shouted. 'Luka, there's a boat!' To his surprise, she did not answer. But when he turned he saw her some way back, crouching down among the trees on the edge of the lakeside.

'Luka,' he called a little angrily, 'why didn't you answer me just now?' Still she didn't speak, but only stared at him.

Thomas reached her quickly. 'What is it? What's the matter? Are you frightened because of the boat?'

'No, it's that,' she muttered, nodding towards the lake. Her heels were dug into the soft earth under the trees, and her hands pressed down on it, as if desperate for the contact.

'The lake?'

Luka nodded. 'Other clans use boats, and fish here, but we never do. For us it's a place of the dead. I hate it, Thomas. It's too open, there's too much sky over it.'

Thomas sat down beside her. 'I had a friend who was afraid to come into the forest,' he said ruefully. 'It seems funny that you're afraid to leave it.'

'And weren't you afraid of the forest?' Luka asked resentfully.

Thomas laughed. 'The thing that frightened me most was seeing you when you came into the glade that night,' he said.

But Luka would not be comforted. 'I said I'd bring you here, and I have. I told you I'd go no further,' she said, and dug her fingers into the earth near the roots of the willow she was crouching under.

Thomas did not know what to do. He hated to leave her. 'Will you wait for me here then? If I'm not back in two days, you'll know not to wait any more.'

Luka got angrily to her feet. 'It's not the magician I'm afraid of,' she said, eyes blazing. 'You don't believe me, but it's true.'

Thomas put out a hand to touch her arm. 'I know you're not afraid of him,' he said gently. 'I am, but I'm the one that has to go. I'm sorry to lose your company, that's all.'

She turned away, her face unreadable.

'I have to go,' Thomas repeated. He wanted to say more, but he didn't know how to. 'Keep my pack and things safe for me, won't you?' He let go of her arm and turned back towards the lake.

He walked out as far as the water's edge and watched the boat coming towards him. In the lulls when the wind dropped, he could hear the splashing of the oars in time with the white marks in the grey water. The oarsman had a powerful broad back and a dark head; it must be

Declan, Thomas realised with a sharp shock. As the boat neared the shore, it turned broadside on the choppy waves at the water's edge. Declan shouted something which was snatched away instantly by the wind, but Thomas guessed his meaning and started out to the boat. The water only came up to his knees, but it was very cold and the current was strong. Declan was having to use the oars to keep the boat still.

As Thomas reached it, grasping the hard curved side, he heard splashing behind him. Turning quickly, he saw Luka. She had left the shore and was wading after him to the boat. Her face was set, her eyes fixed straight ahead, as though she dared not look up or down. Her very movements seemed to show how much she loathed the touch of the water. As she reached the boat and clutched its side she called out to Thomas, 'I said at the beginning that I would take you to Midwinter. I haven't completed the bargain yet.'

Thomas could only smile at her and, with Declan's help, he got her into the boat.

Once in the boat Thomas had the chance to thank her, but Luka said nothing. Declan rowed in silence, occasionally grunting with the effort of battling against currents which threatened to drag them off course. He did not look much older than Thomas's vague memory of him; he had always been large and strange. His big lopsided face betrayed no emotion that Thomas could interpret. Only once, as Thomas's gaze accidentally locked with his own, did he seem to smile.

'Do you know what I have come for?' Thomas asked him on impulse.

Declan paused briefly in his rowing. 'I can guess,' he said in his guttural voice.

Thomas was surprised by the calm confidence Declan showed. He had expected a persecuted fool, but maybe in the loneliness of the forest he had healed. Or perhaps Midwinter . . . but Thomas could not bring himself to think about his uncle. He sat back and put his arm round Luka, hoping it would be some comfort, and watched over Declan's shoulder as the shore of the lake grew smaller in the distance. He began to feel curiously suspended, lulled by the rhythm of the boat and the noise of the wind, flecked with icy rain. Then he felt Luka's rigid body shift slightly against his side, and her fear rekindled his own.

The boat was very close to the shore now. Standing behind them at the water's edge was a man dressed in black. His thin face was old and bearded, but Thomas would have known those eyes anywhere. They met his own with disturbing intensity and he turned away. Then, with a hard jolt, the boat ran on to the shore. Declan jumped out to make it fast and Thomas struggled to his feet. A hand reached out from beside the boat to steady him.

'Welcome,' said Midwinter.

Eight

Thomas stepped off the boat and stood face to face with him. Midwinter was smiling. 'I have been expecting you,' he said.

Thomas nodded. 'You told Luka to guide me. But I don't understand how you knew.'

Midwinter laughed. 'I knew you would want to find out the truth. The castle is a place of secrets and silence, isn't it? Sooner or later, I knew you would be drawn to the forest and to me.'

This was disturbing, but Midwinter's appearance was even more so. He seemed almost old. Perhaps it was the strain of study which had lined Midwinter's face and whitened his hair. He still stood erect in his long black gown, as thin and supple as a willow wand, but no one would have taken him for the younger brother of Lord Ortellus.

'And how is my brother?' Midwinter asked, as if reading Thomas's thoughts. 'Everything is well with him and his people I hope?'

'No, everything is far from well. That's why I came. The raiders are besieging the castle. My mother is dead and my father is half mad with grief. And I have something to ask from you. Something to demand.' He amended it sternly, raising his eyes and looking straight at his uncle. His heart was beating very hard, and he only just heard Midwinter say softly, 'Something to demand? And what is that?'

'The thing you stole.' Thomas raised his voice. 'I have come to take back the Sword.'

'What I stole I no longer have,' Midwinter said. 'What I still keep is mine by right.'

'Don't try to distract me with riddles,' Thomas said angrily. 'I know you have the Sword.'

'I do not mean to play games with you,' Midwinter said with a smile. 'I have waited a long time for you to come. I will tell you the truth, Thomas, every particle.'

His gaze was intense and extraordinarily benevolent. Thomas looked away along the shore. 'I have to help Luka,' he said abruptly and walked away.

He went round to the other side of the boat where Luka was still sitting, head lowered, looking down at her hands. As Thomas reached in and touched her arm she gave a start and turned to him, eyes wide with apprehension. 'I'll help you get out,' he reassured her. 'The water isn't deep and it's just a few steps to the shore.'

Luka, however, did not take the hand Thomas offered. She splashed through the water to the security of land. Then defiantly, she raised her head and stared into the wide grey sky. 'Why should I be afraid of it when you aren't?' she asked Thomas.

Thomas smiled ruefully. He nodded towards Midwinter. 'Why should I be afraid of *him* when you aren't? And the more he talks about the truth, the more scared I get.'

Midwinter and Declan had finished their talk. Declan gave a slight bow and turned away, disappearing quickly among the trees that lined the narrow strip of beach. Midwinter came towards Thomas and Luka, his hand extended. 'I have sent Declan ahead to prepare some food. You must be hungry. Will you eat with me, both of you?'

Thomas hesitated, but Luka said at once, 'Of course we will.'

Midwinter smiled at her. 'Welcome. Thank you for bringing Thomas to me.'

Luka smiled back. 'I kept my part of the bargain, I helped him in his hunt. But while I was alone I often sensed you in the forest, watching over me.'

Midwinter paused, then nodded. 'I did not want harm to come to you, Luka, because I could not lift the enchantment all at once.'

They both smiled then, and Thomas, looking from one to the other, had the idea of an exchange taking place which went beyond the words being spoken. When Luka next spoke it was on a different subject. 'What happened to the boy who was with you, that first time? Is he waiting for us somewhere on the island?'

Midwinter put a hand to his face briefly. When he removed it, he looked sadder and more tired. 'That is part of Thomas's story,' he said. 'But shall we eat first? My house is only a little way further.'

It was indeed only a short walk away through the trees. They came to a small clearing, and Thomas, who had been expecting something very much grander and stranger, was surprised to find they were approaching a hut made of logs with a low roof of turf. A stream ran through the glade behind it and the trees around were hung with beehives. Hens scratched and strutted in the dirt, while nearby a goat, tethered to a pole, cropped the grass. Just outside the hut Declan was bending over a pot on the fire. The savoury smell of cooking brought a rush of water into Thomas's mouth. But he could not quite believe that this was how his uncle lived.

He turned to Midwinter, uncertainly. 'Those are real animals, then?'

Midwinter laughed, and looked a little embarrassed. 'Declan has been borrowing them for years. He always tells me they wandered into the forest on their own and needed rescuing, but I suspect him of helping the process a little. No doubt the farmers place the blame on your people, Luka. Still, it means we have good food to offer you.'

He led them to the fire and brought stools for them to sit on. The food, when it was ready, seemed the most delicious Thomas had ever tasted, though it was simple enough, a stew of bacon and winter vegetables, followed by curds and honey, with hot, spiced mead to wash it down. Midwinter served them himself, and Declan sat with them. After they had eaten, Declan produced a bag of chestnuts and set them to roast on the fire.

Thomas felt warm and heavy, almost ready for sleep. For a few minutes, no one spoke. Then Midwinter said, 'It is time, I suppose, to begin my story. Let me tell it like a winter's tale. It's strange enough.

'There were once two brothers living in a castle far from here. The younger of the two grew up to be a soldier with a fine skill at arms and the power to inspire those under his command. The elder took another path, searching among dusty books and manuscripts for a forgotten history, and a lost power.'

'Wait,' Thomas interrupted uneasily. 'You weren't the elder, Midwinter. My father was.'

Midwinter looked at him. 'Listen to the story,' he said quietly. 'Then you may judge its meaning.'

Thomas stared down at the ground, feeling confused and angry. If this was a trick, he wasn't going to be deceived. Nothing Midwinter could say would change his mind about taking back the Sword.

'The two brothers lived together peacefully enough until their father died and it was time for the elder son to inherit. He took power, selfishly perhaps, because he did not wish to have to choose between his researches and his birthright, and he tried to rule his country with half a mind elsewhere. He made his younger brother Captain of the Guard, second in command in all his affairs and for a while both were content. The captain had scope for his practical nature and proved himself to be loyal and trustworthy. People came to him with their petitions in peacetime, and in times of war he led the raids.

'As time went on, Lord Ortellus handed over to him everything but his title and spent his time among his books and his experiments. And still everything went well. Then, in the same year, only a month apart, sons were born to the wives of the two men. The captain began to be troubled. He had power for his own lifetime, all but the name, but his son would not inherit.'

Thomas could not sit still and be silent any longer. 'Are you trying to tell me that my father . . .' he began hotly, but Midwinter silenced him with a movement of his hand.

'Hear the story to the end,' he insisted.

Thomas could do nothing else. He watched Midwinter's face grow yet more grim as he continued.

'The captain looked on his nephew with resentment, with growing hatred, but he dared not hurt him. Instead he began to spread rumours about Lord Ortellus, that he was dabbling in the black arts, that he was dealing with demons. It was an easy matter for the captain to foster discontent among his soldiers and to permit the suggestion that he, who had the burden of power, should have the honour as well. It was not long before the soldiers rose in rebellion.'

Thomas shook his head.

'Believe it,' Midwinter said gently. 'That is what happened. The captain came to his brother like a shocked and innocent man and warned him what was taking place. He offered to provide Lord Ortellus with a horse, give him time to pack a few books, let him out of the castle ahead of the inevitable pursuit. But Midwinter, though foolish in one great matter, was not in small ways a dupe. He had a trusted servant.' Here he looked across at Declan and smiled. 'This servant had heard whispers in corners and knew that a gang of soldiers was waiting with drawn swords down the lonely road the captain had urged them to take. So instead, the two of them formed a plan of their own. While Declan packed, I went to fetch the Sword. It was laughably easy; the castle was in turmoil and a whispered spell confused the sight of those I passed. The other most precious thing I would not abandon was my son.'

'Philip,' Thomas whispered.

Midwinter smiled. It was, Thomas thought, the saddest smile he had ever seen.

'It was Philip I took. But Philip was not my son.'

Thomas felt his breath stop. He could not take his eyes off Midwinter's face.

'You were so alike, almost like twins. You slept in the same room, shared the same nurse. When I came into the room that night, both of you were sleeping. I knew which cot was yours, or so I thought, and I snatched up the baby in it.'

'I know,' Thomas said quietly. 'I remember.'

'Yes, you woke up. You stared up at me so solemnly. I do not know how I did not realise that I had the wrong child in my arms. You always stared at me like that, solemnly. I spent so little time with you, another neglect.'

'Then, you are my father? And Lord Ortellus . . .'

'Is your uncle and a usurper. Through my stupid haste I left you a hostage in his hands. There is nothing in my life I regret more.'

Thomas got to his feet and walked away. He felt his whole life had been taken away from him. His father was not his father. Lord Ortellus was a usurper and Midwinter owned the Sword. It did not seem possible, yet he had to believe it.

That's why I could never please my father, he told himself. He wanted his own son, he wanted Philip. That's why they all watched me and kept thinking I was like Midwinter. That's why my mother . . . But that thought was too painful to finish. She was not his mother, and yet he still loved her as though she was.

He turned violently on his heel and walked back to the others. 'What happened to my mother?' he almost shouted at Midwinter. 'If what you say is true, what happened to her?'

'She died the day you were born,' Midwinter said quietly. 'I'm sorry, Thomas.'

There was nothing, then. 'It's not fair,' Thomas whispered, and began to cry like a child.

It was Luka who came to comfort him, hugging him in her thin green arms and stroking his hair gently. 'Don't cry, Thomas, or I'll cry too.'

'I'm all right. Honestly, I'm all right.' After a little while, Thomas wiped his face on his sleeve and walked back with her to the fire. 'What happened to Philip?' he asked, his voice still a little shaky.

'Philip died,' Declan said sadly from the other side of the circle.

Midwinter confirmed it. 'He did not live beyond his tenth year. He never forgot the castle, he belonged there. But how could I take him back? I did not realise my mistake until we were on the outskirts of the forest. And I was afraid for you. If my brother got his son back safely, what would he do to you? So I kept Philip and tried to make a son of him. But he took no interest in the magic arts. He would not learn to read. He ran wild all over the island, making animal traps and inventing weapons to play with. Sometimes, to comfort him, I let him handle the Sword. But it was never enough. He died with his face to the north, where his father was.'

Thomas was silent. He tried to imagine Philip's life here alone with Midwinter and Declan in the secret world of the forest. If it had been his own life, would he have pined for the coldness of the castle, for the sword drill and for raids?

'You should have come back for me. I would have learnt everything you could teach me. I would have been your son.'

Midwinter looked at him in grief and pity. 'Is it too late for you to be my son?'

Thomas spoke slowly. 'When I was at the castle I thought it was my fault I was different. I didn't know anyone else felt what I felt, or dreamt the same dreams. I belong with you. I want to stay.'

Midwinter stood and held out his arms and Thomas stepped forward into his warm and strong embrace. 'Stay,' Midwinter said, 'for as long as you want and can. Everything here is yours.'

'Thank you,' Thomas murmured. When he moved away, he saw his father, too, was weeping.

They had talked away most of the day. Above them, the first stars were appearing in the early evening sky.

'You should rest now, you and Luka both,' Midwinter said. 'In the morning we can speak again, about the future as well as the sad past.'

Luka got to her feet, yawning. 'Everything in the forest must sleep, they say. Well, I shan't have any trouble.'

And Thomas, yawning in sympathy, felt fatigue settle round him like a heavy cloak. Midwinter smiled and nodded to Declan, who got up to take them into the hut.

'Nothing will come near to disturb your dreams,' he said. 'I will stay here and watch for a while.'

Nine

When Thomas woke up next morning he opened his eyes on to the semi-darkness of the hut.

'Luka?' he called softly without moving, but there was no reply. He turned and saw that the other bed was empty and the hammocks Declan had slung from the roof for himself and Midwinter were packed away. Thomas stretched his limbs against the soft feather mattress. He had slept well and it was good to feel warm and safe. He could see the bunches of long feathery herbs hanging from the roof to dry and the oddly-shaped flasks and still, ranged on the trestle-table in front of the stove. Midwinter's books, four or five heavy volumes bound in leather, lay stacked on a shelf above the table. The air smelt of wood-smoke and spices. It was a strange place to feel at home in, Thomas thought, but that was how he felt.

At last he threw off the sheepskin that covered him and reached down for his boots. When he opened the door of the hut, the light made him blink and for a moment he could see nothing. It was a fine cold day. The sky above was clear and blue and the trees and ground before him glittered with frost. His breath smoked out in front of him and his lungs expanded to take in the clean cold air.

'Declan?' he called out. 'Luka? Is anyone around?' Declan came suddenly towards him from behind the hut. 'You gave me a start!' Thomas grinned at him.

Declan gave a slow smile. 'We have been up a good two hours.'

'Can you tell me where my father is?'

Declan pointed. 'Out over that way. You can have some breakfast if you wait for me to finish with the animals.'

'That's all right, I'll go and see if I can find him.' He set off with a wave and a nod, his boots crunching over the frosty ground.

He heard the others before he saw them, some way into the trees beyond the stream. His instinct was to stop and listen. Luka's voice was raised in a high-pitched sort of singing, accompanied by a rhythmic stamping of feet. When she paused, Midwinter's voice took over, echoing the same phrases. Afraid they would stop if they heard him, Thomas crept forward as silently as he could to find them in a little clearing.

'So the huntsmen move into a wide circle,' Luka called out, 'and the deer wheels around . . .' She turned swiftly, fingers hooked behind her head to imitate horns, feet stepping in a quick delicate movement to show the terror of the deer. 'The huntsmen advance,' said Midwinter, striding forward and raising his right arm. 'The spears fly through the air . . .'

Luka began a wild ululation in her throat that stopped abruptly. 'And the deer is brought down,' she said in a stricken voice, lowering her hands.

Midwinter came towards her. 'You know more than the dancer,' he said quietly. 'You know more than the hunter. You know it from the inside now.'

'Yes,' said Luka fiercely. 'But I did not choose to know it. That is the difference between my knowledge and yours, magician.'

Thomas moved so that he could see his father's face. 'You are right,' Midwinter said. 'Yet even the knowledge I have was bought at a price.'

Luka was silent, looking at him. 'I have drunk at a stream in which a trout played,' she said at last, 'but it was not a trout's mind that looked out of that eye. I have wandered in the forest at night when a white owl was crying, and his cry seemed to me to have something human in it. And once, as I lay in a clearing, a fieldmouse came trembling to my side. I could have crushed it with a movement.'

'But you did not,' said Midwinter.

'I did not,' Luka agreed, 'for I knew it was you that was near me.'

Thomas turned and began to creep away as silently as he could. He felt ashamed to have overheard what was surely private. At the same time he felt desolate. Luka and his father belonged to the forest and to each other in a way he felt he could never share. He might have spent his childhood here, but all he had instead were a few words learnt out of books. He wanted to be by himself for a little while, to sort out his feelings, but the others had already seen him.

'Thomas!' Luka called out joyfully. 'You're up at last. Have you had something to eat?'

'No.' Thomas returned her smile with something of an effort. 'I wanted to find you first.'

'Well, you were walking in the wrong direction for that,' Luka retorted. She ran to catch up with him and linked her arm through his. He wondered what else had happened to make her so happy.

'Midwinter has been telling me about the old magic,' she said. 'My people know the powers of the forest, but they do not remember all that the ancestors knew. But things are written down in Midwinter's books from the days when your people and mine met without fear.'

'And it seems that I have acquired an apprentice,' Midwinter said, smiling.

'Good for you, Luka,' Thomas said, trying hard to feel pleased.

Midwinter looked at him shrewdly, and in a moment had taken Luka's place at his side. 'I think you already know most of what Luka will be learning. My apprenticeship took place in the castle library. I memorised everything I could, useful or not. Did you ever come across that fat red book, what was it called . . .'

'With the spoilt gold tooling and a torn cover?' Thomas said eagerly. 'Lord Savvas's journal?'

Midwinter nodded. 'That's the one. I copied hundreds of extracts from there. I still have them with me. His fire spell, that he got from Luka's clan . . .'

'And the healing spells, for fevers and infections . . .'

'All lost to us now,' Luka said sadly. 'I don't know any of it.'

'But what about all the rest of the things he wrote down?' Thomas said, laughing suddenly. 'That recipe for baking snails in clay and honey, and all that nonsense about how to breed smaller horses so you could have two-storey stables!'

' "My observations have led me to conclude . . ." ' Midwinter intoned with mock solemnity. 'He just wrote down all the nonsense anybody told him, I suppose. Anybody and everybody, in Rossendale and outside. But there's nothing the matter with his magic.'

Thomas felt suddenly happy, remembering all the books he had opened that his father had handled and pored over before him. 'I had to find my own way,' Midwinter said, looking at him. 'Just like you, Thomas.' Before Thomas could reply, a shout interrupted them. It was an urgent, almost desperate noise.

'Someone at the landing place,' Midwinter said. 'The green people cross the river when they need help from me.'

Together they hurried down to the little bay. On the flat muddy shore a boat was drawn up, and beside it stood a man who raised both arms to wave, then ran towards them. 'It's my little son. He fell from a tree two days ago while playing.'

Looking beyond him, Thomas could see a woman still sitting in the boat, bending to cradle a child lying across her lap.

'His arm is badly broken, and none of our herbs have brought down his fever,' the man continued, his eyes fixed imploringly on Midwinter. 'Surely you will help us?'

'Willingly,' Midwinter said.

The boy's mother looked up as they approached. She had been crying, but now she managed a faint smile.

'What is your son's name?' Midwinter asked.

'Mansa,' she whispered.

'Sparrow,' Luka murmured to Thomas. 'It's a nickname. In their clan he's too young to have his full name yet.'

'Help me to lift him down,' Midwinter said.

Gently they laid him on the ground with a blanket under him. He groaned faintly, but did not wake. He was about four or five, and the huge wad of splints and wrappings around his injured arm made him look skinny and frail. His mother came to kneel beside him. 'We can't get him to take any water,' she told them. 'And if he opens his eyes he does not seem to know us.' Frightened, she bent over her son again, murmuring his name and pushing his hair back from his forehead.

Midwinter took Thomas aside. 'We spoke of healing spells,' he said quietly. 'Do you want to attempt this?' Thomas took a sharp breath, then nodded.

Midwinter smiled, then took his hand and led him forward. 'This is my son,' he told Mansa's parents. 'He will heal Mansa.'

Thomas stooped over the child and very gently freed the wrappings around his injured arm. A faint sheen of sweat coated Mansa's fine-boned face; he cried out but did not wake. The fracture was ugly, the flesh bruised and torn and the bone projecting from the skin. Thomas felt a moment of self-consciousness and doubt. He had to forget the boy's parents standing behind him full of trust and hope. He had to forget Luka was there, willing him to succeed. Above all he had to forget his new love for Midwinter, and the desire to prove himself a worthy son. He emptied his mind of everything but the words of healing, and held his hands over Mansa and began.

He chanted quietly, relying on the spell itself to tell him where to touch the boy and with what pressure. His fingers began to tingle and burn as they found the source of the fever. His voice rose as he began to draw the fever out and he felt a pain as though he was thrusting his hands into a fire. Then it was gone, dispersed in the wind, and Mansa let out a gentle sigh, and curled on to his side.

However, Thomas still had to set the arm. He held his hand over the snapped bone and eased it back into place. His hands grew warm again as he began the work of healing the wound. And suddenly he was aware of a voice beside his own, hands held over his, strengthening and sharing the magic. Midwinter was kneeling beside him. Together father and son chanted the words of power, reconnecting bone with bone, renewing the broken vessels and mending the torn flesh. The gashed edges of the wound rose and smoothed out. Then the green skin crept over it, and only the faintest of scars remained on Mansa's smooth arm.

Thomas got to his feet feeling drained, but exultant. Midwinter rose more slowly. He looked down at the sleeping boy, and said to his mother, 'The arm will be weak for a little while yet. Make sure he doesn't go climbing any more trees!'

Then he turned to Thomas. There was a look of wonder in his eyes the boy did not understand until Midwinter spoke. 'I did not have such power at your age. I thought you might need my help for the healing, but your own strength was enough. I am proud of you, Thomas.'

Thomas felt too much to be able to speak. He could only look at his father, and through that look show him that, at last, he had found where he belonged. Then Mansa's parents were crowding round him with their thanks and praise, and Mansa himself had woken, staring round in bewilderment, and there was no chance of any more private talk between father and son.

When at last they were free to make their way back to the hut, Luka deliberately ran ahead a little way. Thomas was the first to speak. 'Rossendale seems so far away now. I wish I could stay in the forest with you and never go back.'

'But that isn't the reason you came,' Midwinter said gently.

'I know,' Thomas said with a rueful look. 'But everything's changed now. I don't want to take the Sword back just to help my usurping uncle drive out the raiders. If I do, I'll be agreeing to the lie that the Sword is rightfully his.'

'Does that matter so much if it brings an end to the suffering of Rossendale?' Midwinter asked.

'But it won't,' Thomas said, passionately. 'The raiders will just come back again. If all I do is take the Sword back to the castle, the raids will continue and the pattern will never be broken. My father . . . my uncle will lead the raids until he dies, and then it will be my turn. I don't want to go back to that. It'll be as if the forest and magic never existed, as if I never came here.' He looked at Midwinter and added, 'It frightens me. I feel as if I have just one chance to do what is right, to change things. Only I don't yet see exactly what to do.'

Midwinter stooped to pick up a stone, turning it in his hand a moment before he spoke. 'The strange thing about the Sword is that nobody seems sure exactly where it came from. You know the stories. There's always the idea that it came from outside Rossendale, from across the sea.'

'You mean that it doesn't really belong to us?' Thomas said in a voice full of hope and excitement. 'Of course! I had almost forgotten. When I heard the raiders talking, they said the Sword was theirs. That is why they have been demanding it. Not to crush us, but to unite themselves under one leader. If Erik returns home with the Sword, they have no reason to come to Rossendale again. There will be no more raids. I have to make sure of that.'

He spoke so loudly that Luka ran back to see what was happening. 'Think of it, Luka,' Thomas said, turning to her with shining eyes. 'If I could give the Sword back to the raiders, there would be peace at last. It would be like the Rossendale of the old times. We could go exploring instead of fighting. Your people and my people would learn magic together.'

But Midwinter shook his head. 'Nothing is certain,' he insisted gently. 'Any choice brings a risk with it. What if the raiders are so full of pride and battle fury that they do not want the killing to stop? What if, when they have the Sword, they use it to cut Rossendale to pieces?'

Thomas shivered and fell silent.

Luka asked uncertainly, 'But is it really up to Thomas to decide? He isn't yet the chief of his people.'

Thomas looked at Midwinter. 'Luka's right. You are still Lord of Rossendale, not me, nor my uncle in the castle.'

But Midwinter shook his head. 'I have had my chance. I was not a good ruler, Thomas. I did not use what I gained from my books for the service of men. I was too selfish, too absorbed in my own desires. In the old times, you know, it was only possible to spend a little time in the forest. A prince always had to return home and put his wisdom to use.'

'Then I have to go back.' Thomas looked into his father's face. 'I have to go back, and I have to decide about the Sword.'

Midwinter nodded. 'I know it is hard,' he said gently. 'You are my son, but you are my brother's also, since he has had the rearing of you.

There was a time when I found that very bitter, but now it makes me glad. Take the best you know of both of us, Thomas, and you will save Rossendale.'

They had reached the clearing near the hut. Declan was cooking what smelt deliciously like eggs and bacon, but Thomas had little appetite. He was too preoccupied with all that had happened, and with the uncertain future.

'You're very quiet, Thomas,' Luka said at last.

'I was wondering how long it will take me to get home. The journey here must have taken almost a week.'

'Don't trouble too much about that,' Midwinter said. He stood up. 'Come with me, my son. It's time for me to show you something.'

Thomas followed him towards the hut. Once inside, Midwinter went over to a dark, heavily-carved chest. 'I have kept this for many years, now it is time to hand it on.'

He opened the chest and drew out something wrapped in a blue silk cloth. He held it out to Thomas in the flat of his two hands.

'Is it the Sword?' Thomas whispered.

'The Sword and something else.'

Thomas took the bundle and laid it carefully on the table, then turned to open the door behind him a little wider to increase the light. 'Oh, but it's beautiful!' he exclaimed as he unwrapped the silk. 'I did not imagine it would be so beautiful.'

The handle of the Sword was of silver, smooth to the touch, and the scabbard was of enamelled gold in an intricate pattern of trees and birds. He drew out the Sword and held it up. It was as terrible as it was lovely, heavy and yet balanced in his hand.

'I lay no condition on your stewardship,' Midwinter said. 'You must decide where it rightfully belongs.'

Thomas put the Sword back in its scabbard and laid it down. 'You said there was something else.' He felt in the blue silk wrapping and brought out a small, hard, oval shape. As he turned it over he realised what it was.

'Your mother made me promise to keep it for you.' There were tears in Midwinter's eyes.

Thomas looked down at the miniature. It showed the head and shoulders of a woman, dark-haired and fair-skinned. She was smiling at him from the distance, her eyes full of warm intelligence as if she knew and loved him. 'I wish she hadn't died.'

'She fought for her life. She didn't want to leave you.'

There was a fine gold chain attached to the little miniature. Thomas slipped it over his head and pushed it down under his shirt. 'Thank you,' he said simply.

Midwinter put a hand on his shoulder. 'Are you ready to go back?'

Slowly Thomas nodded. 'But I've only just found you. It's hard to go back and leave you and Luka behind.'

'Even Luka will not stay with me for long. She too must return to her people to teach them what has been forgotten. Magic is not a private pleasure, Thomas. That was the mistake I made. You belong to your people, and their need is pressing.'

Thomas looked stricken.

'I know it is hard,' Midwinter said gently. 'But you will come back. The forest is always here for you. And I do not mean to end my days without seeing you again.'

They went out of the hut together, Thomas wearing the Sword on his belt. Luka ran forward and kissed him.

Declan stood up and grinned. 'It's done, then?' he asked.

'It's done,' Midwinter said. 'And now it's time for Thomas to go back.'

'He'll have a hard trudge of it,' Declan said, 'unless you have something in mind.'

'Oh, I do,' said the magician.

Midwinter moved towards the fire. Declan and Luka watched him expectantly. He stood warming his hands for a moment, saying nothing. Then he turned to Luka. 'How old is the forest, would you say, in the estimate of your people?'

Luka showed surprise. 'Thousands and thousands of years. We don't count a time before the forest.'

'Yet there was such a time,' Midwinter said. 'There was a time when this valley was under water and the sea next to Ortellus Castle was a meadow. That was a time, Luka, when your people lived in another forest, and the forest here was more like a swamp. Strange animals lived in it, lizards bigger than wolves, and huge birds with leather wings and razor teeth.'

Luka shivered. 'Do your books tell you such things?'

'My books and my own wits,' Midwinter replied. 'Under the forest lie the bones of all its dead. I have seen strange bones in this ground, Luka, bones of creatures no longer seen above it. But they had existence once, and my books have shown me how to give them existence again, for a little time.'

He held his hands towards the fire again. 'Warmth for old bones,' he murmured. 'Fire to stir them and a skin to cover them.'

He took off his cloak and laid it on the ground. Declan, with a sharp gesture, motioned the others away. Thomas watched as his father began to speak in a loud commanding voice. He could not understand the words, and at first he thought nothing was happening. The cloak shivered slightly near Midwinter's feet. Thomas rubbed his eyes, looked away, and looked back. As Midwinter stepped quickly backward, the cloak shook more violently. It was shimmering and quivering like a liquid rushing up to the boil.

At a word, it moved out of its own boundaries, flooding the fire and lapping the ground at Midwinter's feet. His hands and his chant controlled it, his face intent. Then the tone of his speaking changed, became quieter and more rhythmical. The shape on the ground seemed to grow solid again, by this time it was huge and definite. Thomas could make out the span of two great wings, a beak and, where the fire had been, a dark stain in the shape of a heart.

Midwinter gave a sharp command and the ground beneath the bird-shape seemed to gather and bulge. Suddenly the head reared up like a living thing; the neck twisted round and the beak opened, displaying small savage teeth. A cold yellow eye regarded them all with disdain. Next the wings shook themselves free and last, the slim body and strong clawed legs. The creature stood and threw back its head, calling back along the centuries to its kind in a high-pitched yearning cry that echoed through the trees and across the lake and brought no answer.

Thomas turned to Midwinter in disbelief. 'You don't expect me to ride home on *that*?'

'It will bear you to Rossendale in a few hours. Don't worry. It will not take you anywhere but the castle. I have limited its purpose.'

'You might have limited its teeth,' Luka muttered.

'But what'll happen to it when I get to the castle?' Thomas asked, trying not to jump out of the way as the thing turned its neck and stared at him. 'You can't leave it to fly around wild.'

'I won't,' Midwinter said impatiently. 'I haven't. You can't bring something back like this and have it live. It isn't really alive now.'

Thomas was scarcely encouraged by this. 'You mean it could just fall to bits while I'm flying on its back?'

'Of course not,' Midwinter said, even more shortly.

He went right up to the creature and laid his hand on its smooth dark neck. It accepted his touch, its big wings vibrating gently against the ground. Midwinter's head was at its shoulder level, and had it wished, it could have taken him into its powerful jaws and torn him to pieces.

'This is where you sit,' the magician said, turning to Thomas. 'Up here on the shoulders, so you can keep hold around its neck. If you get sleepy, sing or something to keep yourself awake. I can't protect you from the consequences of falling off.'

'I don't think there's any danger of my sleeping,' Thomas said. He gritted his teeth and walked up to the creature. Each of its wings was as long as the span of the boy's extended arms. It fixed him with its yellow eyes and waited.

'How do I . . .' Thomas began, but before he could finish his sentence, Midwinter had hoisted him up on to the creature's back.

Thomas knew a moment of total panic as his fingers clutched the giant creature's neck. But the smooth column of neck-muscle under the warm skin did not feel so strangely different from a horse's, only thicker. He pulled himself upright and felt the creature's shoulders adjust to his weight. It was not going to throw him off. He opened his eyes and looked along the curve of the neck out over the small earless head. Beneath him, powerful wing-muscles gently fanned. He thought with sudden exhilaration of the flight to come.

'Thomas!' Luka called up to him. 'Thomas, aren't you afraid?'

'No!' he cried. 'Goodbye, Luka. Goodbye, Declan!'

Then it was time to say goodbye to his father. The sudden pain he felt made it hard to breathe, let alone speak.

'Goodbye, my son.'

Midwinter spoke with such sadness that Thomas could hardly bear it. Tears pricked his eyes as he replied. 'I will come back. Nothing but death can stop me.'

Then the creature under him began to move. Slowly at first it stalked across the clearing, then gathering speed, it began to run, its wings fully extended and beating hard. With a leap of the heart, Thomas felt it leave the ground. They soared steeply upward over the trees and wheeled round again to where the others stood with upturned faces below. Thomas waved and shouted, though his words were snatched away by the blustering wind. 'Goodbye, goodbye, I will come back, I promise!'

He could just make out their faces. Luka's was small and anxious, her arm raised to wave frantically. Declan was smiling as if taking pleasure in the grace and power of the creature in the air. But Midwinter stood a little apart from both of them. His eyes were fixed on Thomas as though he could not bear to lose sight of him again so soon. With an effort he roused himself and raised his hand in a last farewell. Then the giant creature wheeled northward across the lake, and Thomas began his journey home.

Ten

He did not know how long they had been flying. Whenever he looked down, it was still to see the forest, black and green and brown, criss-crossed by streams like the leading in stained glass. Mostly he did not look down but lay forward with his face pressed against the strong neck of the creature. Even in that position he could not escape the battering of the wind, which froze his hands into claws and stung his eyes, blinding him with tears. Blood drummed in his ears and he fought to get his breath in the brutal wind. He had imagined flight as a calm progress through the silent spaces of the sky, but it was not, it was a battle in which he had to trust in the power and sureness of the creature striving to make its way through the currents of the air.

Then he could see open glades, and then fields interspersed with little woods and copses. The road appeared and disappeared like a broken thread. They passed over a shuttered farm and the fields grew wider, brown and green and flecked with dirty white. As they passed another farm, Thomas was suddenly convinced he recognised it as the place he and Billy had seen the raider. Billy would be back at the castle now, unless he was hiding in a village somewhere, afraid to face Margaret Claypole's wrath at him coming home alone. Anything, Thomas thought, so long as he wasn't lying in a ditch somewhere with a raider's knife through his body.

His mind dwelt uneasily on Billy's fate until, to his left, there came a glimpse of the coast and the pewter-grey sheen of the sea. The creature began to climb and bank to the right, rising above a bony ridge of land that Thomas recognised. It had taken them many hours to trek along it, leading the horses. The road was down below him, between the ridge and the sea, and they were starting to pass villages whose names he knew, Sealham and Saltbeck, Dunby and Whitham; villages he had never visited but had inked painstakingly on to one of the maps Dr Castang made him copy. He was flying above a giant map of Rossendale, only he couldn't see the thing that concerned him most, the raider ships out at sea. Were they still concentrated in Ortellus Harbour, laying a blockade against the castle? Soon he would know, for he recognised the outline of the hills they were flying towards. It was the familiar view from his own window, though the angle was different. They were almost home. He reached with numb fingers for the Sword at his side and thought with pride of what Margaret Claypole would say to him.

They reached the top of the ridge. The whole bay was spread out before them; the dark grey bulk of the castle and the curve of the harbour wall, with the half-ruined cluster of village houses. Out in the middle of the harbour was the massed flotilla of the raiders' ships. The flying creature started its descent. It flew lower in narrowing circles and Thomas, clutching hard round its neck, watched the castle grow bigger beneath them.

Suddenly there was movement on the ground; a man ran into the castle courtyard, pointing upwards and yelling. Thomas was too high to hear him, but he could just make out his open upturned mouth. Others quickly followed, twenty or thirty of them, soldiers pouring into the courtyard. As the creature skimmed the top of the watch-tower something whistled through the air close to the top of Thomas's head. An arrow, he realised in cold surprise. They thought his arrival was some sorcery of the raiders!

He was close enough now to hear the confused shouting of orders and alarms, to see the drawn weapons of the men on the ground and their faces, white with shock. The creature was slowing, gracefully gliding down into the courtyard at the furthest point from the soldiers. For a few moments it hovered, wings beating hard, then it landed deftly, absorbing the shock of the contact into its strong clawed legs. Thomas reached upward and patted the creature's head as he might a horse's, and it responded with a kind of hissing whistle and stretched its neck with pleasure. Across the courtyard the soldiers gripped their swords and waited.

Thomas dared not move either. He craned forward, looking for any face he recognised. He did not want to die, mistaken for a raider in the courtyard of his own castle.

'Where's the captain?' he called out to them. 'It's the captain I want to speak to.'

At a word from behind them, the ranks of soldiers parted and the Captain of the Guard stepped forward. He looked thinner than Thomas remembered and his face under its new growth of beard was grey with fatigue. 'Who are you and what do you want?' he demanded roughly.

Thomas called in a loud voice across the courtyard, 'You know me, Captain, or you should.'

The captain studied him with deliberation for a moment. 'No, I do not know you. State your business quickly, or my men will make an end of you, sorcery or not.'

Thomas's fear turned to anger at this. He could not believe the captain did not recognise him, and began to suspect him of some treachery. 'My name is Thomas Ortellus,' he said loudly. 'And my business is with Lord Ortellus, not with you.'

There was an uneasy stirring and some talk among the soldiers at the captain's back. 'Thomas Ortellus is dead,' the captain said impatiently. 'His servant came back and told us so.'

'You mean Billy's here?' In his relief and eagerness to hear more, Thomas got down from the shoulders of the giant bird and walked towards them.

'He came back yesterday,' the captain said. 'But even if you are Thomas Ortellus, back from the dead on death's creature there, Lord Ortellus will not see you. He sees no one now, except me.'

'No, he keeps safe in his room, while the rest of us starve or are picked off one by one,' a soldier called out, while the others nodded and murmured their agreement.

'Well, if Lord Ortellus won't see me,' Thomas said, trying to keep his temper, 'where is Margaret Claypole? She will have been waiting anxiously for my return.'

The captain smiled. It was not a pleasant smile. 'She was sent down to the village by Lord Ortellus to tend the sick there. A fever has broken out and a lot of them are dying. If she hasn't caught it herself she'll be helping there still. That's if the raiders didn't catch her on the way.'

Thomas was horrified. But before he could say more, he was startled by a great shout from the soldiers. The captain's gaze, too, shifted past him and the expression on his face changed. He was staring incredulously at the creature. Thomas swung round and gave a great cry of alarm. The creature was collapsing, crumpling in on itself. Its head hung loose and had somehow lost its shape, and its neck was melting back into its body like candle wax. As it flattened on to the ground, sparks and ashes flew up and were carried away on the wind. Its empty skin seemed to shrink and thicken, until all that was left of the creature was a ragged cloak and a few protruding bones.

There was a moment of astonished silence. Then the captain smiled. 'Come here, boy,' he said, motioning Thomas forward with his hand. 'Let's see who you really are, now your sorcery has failed you.'

Thomas felt a moment of pure terror. He knew the captain meant to kill him, and recognise him afterwards. 'I told you who I am,' he shouted. 'And my sorcery has not failed me. Midwinter said he wouldn't leave the creature to fly wild. It was only bones and fire after all.'

The captain's smile disappeared. 'Midwinter? This is his foul trickery?'

Thomas shook his head proudly. 'Neither foul, nor a trick. Billy was wrong, I didn't die. I found out who Midwinter is. And he gave me this!'

Thomas drew the Sword, and before any of them could come after him, he backed quickly away towards the door that led to the great hall.

The air of the hall was damp and had a thin sour smell as though nothing good had been eaten there for some time. Thomas quickly crossed to the stairs and began to climb. When he reached the door, he knocked loudly, but there was no answer. He knocked again, and when there was still no answer he turned the heavy handle and went inside.

The man he had called his father was standing near the narrow window on the other side of the room. He had his back to Thomas and gave no sign of having heard him come in. It was late afternoon and the light was fading, bleaching the colour from the tapestries on the wall and the rich curtains of the bed. Thomas waited, and the stillness grew heavy, and the man across the room stood without moving, as if enchanted. Quietly Thomas walked across and touched his arm. Lord Ortellus spun round angrily, but the anger fled from his face to be replaced by confusion.

'Thomas. The boy lied then, when he told me you were dead.'

'As you see, I'm alive.'

'He said you went into the forest.' Lord Ortellus stared at Thomas as if he still could not believe it. 'But I suppose you lost courage and found your own way home.'

'No. I found Midwinter.'

There was a silence. Thomas saw his uncle sway slightly. His face betrayed nothing, but it was as if his body had sustained a heavy blow. 'You know, then,' he said.

'I know.' Thomas tried to control his anger. 'And my father has given me the Sword.'

He held it high up in the dying light, and Lord Ortellus stretched out his hand with a cry of astonishment. Thomas was afraid he was going to snatch it away, but instead he touched the flat of the blade with awe.

'Such a beautiful, dangerous thing. I always wanted it to be mine. Even when I was a very small child, I wanted nothing else. But Midwinter was born first. And so the Sword remained his, however far he retreated into his books and his dreams.' He let his hand drop and looked at Thomas, his eyes now full of pain and rage. 'Midwinter was no ruler! The honour was his, and the work and the worry were mine. I deserved what I took, if any man deserved it. And I did not plan to kill him, whatever he has told you. There is a little island a mile off the coast, where he could have lived under guard with you and his books and his dreams. I would not have harmed him!'

'But why the pretence?' Thomas could not keep the pain out of his own voice as he spoke. 'Why bring me up as your son, when you didn't love me?'

Lord Ortellus hesitated. 'It was not an honourable thing we did. And Midwinter's revenge was savage. No one wanted to remember the pain and shame of that night. So you became my son, and I became Lord, and Midwinter's name disappeared from the Chronicles. Sometimes I almost forgot that the truth was . . . otherwise. Only that space on the wall down in the hall and the pain in your mother's eyes kept the memory.' He smiled a little and looked at Thomas. 'And you, with your dreams and your awkwardness. My son, and not my son.' He paused and a terrible look of hope entered his face. 'What happened to Philip?'

It was a bitter moment for Thomas. 'Philip died in the forest when he was still little. But Midwinter did not kill him. He didn't mean to take him. It was me he wanted.'

There was a silence. Then Lord Ortellus began to laugh. It was a harsh mirthless sound with more pain in it than Thomas could bear. 'So it is a farce we have been living through, and not a tragedy,' Lord Ortellus said. 'Midwinter took Philip by mistake? I am glad his mother did not live to know it. It would have driven her mad.'

Anger boiled up inside Thomas. 'You were the one to blame for that, not me! And don't tell me you didn't mean to kill my father. You would never have felt safe with him alive!'

Lord Ortellus shrugged. 'Perhaps you are right. So what will you do now, Thomas? Kill me with the Sword you are gripping so tightly? I tell you, I will offer no resistance.'

Thomas had not realised he was so close to violence. He lowered the Sword and said quietly, 'I would never willingly hurt you. You have been my father for most of my life.'

'And you have been my son,' said Lord Ortellus. There was pride and affection in his voice, and the look he gave Thomas was full of regret and sadness. 'Forgive me for failing you, I thought I was strong enough. I thought I had only to will a thing for it to become the truth. I willed myself to be Lord, and I willed myself to be your father. But there was emptiness at the heart of all of it. The Sword has come back too late for me, Thomas. The dream is over. I am not Lord of Rossendale. If Midwinter has given you the Sword, it is for you to use.'

Thomas put a hand upon his arm. 'I am your heir as well as his. Whatever I am, whatever I dare to do, it comes from the strength of you both.'

Lord Ortellus smiled. 'Thank you. That is more than I deserve. So what now, Thomas? I will have you proclaimed my successor in this next hour. You have proved yourself, and the people will readily accept you. You can be leading an attack against the raiders before dawn.'

Thomas hesitated for only a moment. 'No, Uncle. The time for killing is over. I did not bring back the Sword to use it against the raiders. It is time to return to the old ways. The wisdom I choose is the wisdom of the forest, not the battlefield. I am going to hand over the Sword.'

Before his uncle could speak, before Thomas could even see a reaction in his face, the door burst open and in rushed the Captain of the Guard. There were a dozen soldiers at his back, and his own sword was drawn. He came forward with an angry cry, and Thomas found himself surrounded.

'My Lord, has this boy dared to trouble you? We have been searching the castle for him.' He turned to Thomas and said curtly, 'Hand over the Sword, if it is indeed the Sword and not another of your sorceror's tricks. I am the one who acts for Lord Ortellus. You have no business here.'

Thomas looked beyond him at the soldiers for a moment, and then he laughed. 'You hope that by snatching the Sword from me you will snatch their hearts as well? But Captain, your men have known me from when I was a tiny child. They know whose son I really am. They know I am Midwinter's heir. You may act for my uncle, but you do not act for the Lord of Rossendale. Now go, on his authority and my uncle's, and proclaim that I am taking up my inheritance.'

The captain was silenced. He could only turn to Lord Ortellus and seek confirmation. After a long moment, to Thomas's joy and relief, Lord Ortellus nodded. 'Thomas is Lord of Rossendale. It is time for the truth to be restored.'

As he looked at Thomas there was both weariness and pride in his expression. 'I do not understand what you mean to do. But I remember the stories Midwinter used to tell me when we were boys. I used to wish such things could be true, until I grew to be a soldier. May your dreams not play you false as mine did, Thomas. May you succeed in bringing peace and ruling wisely. All that is left for me to do is to visit the forest. Before I die I want to see the grave of my son.'

'The forest will help you to understand. You will see there is a better way than the life of raiding.'

'Not for me,' said his uncle with a sad smile. 'I am too old to learn it.'

Thomas turned to the captain. 'Now that you know I have the authority to act, I trust you will obey me. If not, I can call on another man in your place.'

Stiffly, the captain dropped down on one knee. 'What are your instructions?' he demanded in a choked voice.

Thomas smiled ruefully. He did not expect the captain to stay in his service more than one day, once he heard the orders he was about to give. 'After you have made the proclamation, after the people know that I am Lord, I want you to go down to the shore and seek a parlay with the raiders. Tomorrow, at noon, we will make peace with them. Tell them I am coming to hand over the Sword.'

The captain looked at him. 'There is not to be an attack?'

'No attack. No killing. We will discuss the terms of reparations, and draw up a treaty to bring an end to the raids. Then the raiders can return to their farms and villages and our men can return to theirs.'

'You have your orders, man,' said Lord Ortellus impatiently to the captain. 'Do you accept them or not?'

The habit of obedience was strong in the captain, upset only by the confusions of the last few days. Slowly he nodded. 'But do you think the raiders can be trusted? Why should they make a permanent peace for the sake of the Sword?'

'Because for them the Sword means peace; peace among all the islands, and they will not have to look to the raids any more to unite them,' Thomas said. 'Tonight, after dinner, you and Dr Castang can help me draw up the terms of our treaty. For the present, the only other thing I want you to do is to send someone down to the village to find Margaret Claypole. Oh, and if you know where Billy is, tell him I want to see him.'

As the captain turned to go, Thomas sighed with relief. If the captain obeyed him, so would the soldiers. The first, most difficult part of his task was accomplished.

It was late before Billy came. Thomas was lying on his bed, an inch of candle on the table beside him, trying to keep awake. The knock on the door was so timid, so uncertain, that at first he wasn't sure he had heard anything at all. 'Come in,' he called, getting to his feet.

Billy closed the door quietly behind him, but stayed close to it. His eyes didn't quite meet Thomas's as he said, 'They told me you wanted to see me.'

Billy's shyness made Thomas shy too. He nodded without speaking and Billy, misunderstanding his silence, flushed red. 'I can understand it if you're angry. I should never have let you rush off into the forest like that. But I waited for you all day and the next night. I even went in a little way myself, only I was scared of getting lost. After that, all I could do was come back. I was sure you were dead by then.'

Thomas just grabbed him, half hug, half wrestling hold. 'Don't be stupid,' he said, after they had laughed and pushed each other away. 'I was the one throwing stones, not you. I wanted to kill you for what you said, but that was because deep down I knew you were right. Lord Ortellus had his reasons to resent me. I only found out what they were when I met Midwinter.'

'And you got the Sword from him. I didn't believe we would ever find it, let alone bring it back to Rossendale, but you did it. And is it really true that you are Lord Ortellus now?'

'I am.' It was still so new to Thomas that he could not help a brief smile of delight and surprise.

'And that you're giving the Sword to the raiders?'

Thomas nodded. He wondered apprehensively whether Billy would explode in anger, but Billy suddenly looked embarrassed and ill at ease again. 'I should be bowing and calling you "my Lord",' he muttered. 'I'm sorry, Thomas. I'm used to our old way of talking to each other.'

'And if you ever give it up, I'll banish you! Now more than ever, I need friends near me who will tell me the truth. So keep the bowing for later, Billy, and tell me what you think.'

Billy was silent for a moment. 'You talked about it on the journey,' he said slowly. 'How if we handed over the Sword to the raiders, there would be no more fighting. I laughed at that, but I laughed at the idea of us finding the Sword at all. Do you really think it will bring peace and an end to the raids?'

'I know it will,' said Thomas with conviction.

Billy looked at him intently. 'I went to our village before coming to the castle. Everyone's crowded together in half-burnt houses, nothing to eat, frightened of what will happen after dark every night. My brother and my father died the night we left, when the raiders torched the place.

And the sickness is terrible. Only Margaret Claypole came down from the castle to help. And I couldn't help thinking,' he swallowed hard. 'I couldn't help thinking of all the stories my brother told me about what he did when he went on raids. It was no different, Thomas! We do just the same to them as they do to us. We're no better than the raiders. I thought you were a coward for not wanting to fight, but no one who goes into the forest by himself is a coward. You found the Sword and brought it back. I think you know its true home. And whatever path you choose as Lord of Rossendale, I will follow.'

The next day at noon, Thomas Ortellus brought the Sword down to the shore in a procession of trumpeters and banners. Waiting to meet them on the edge of the sea were the Dalmatic islanders. At their head was their leader, Erik, a young man wearing a thin gold circlet. His face was striking, and his deep blue eyes reflected a wisdom older than his years. He stepped away from his followers as the procession came down the path from the castle, holding his arms wide in a gesture of openness and trust.

Both leaders stood in silence while a herald read out the terms of the treaty. Then Thomas held up the Sword. 'We are returning the Sea's Gift. Let there be peace between our peoples.'

Erik looked at the Sword in silence for a moment. 'I have given you my word. It will be binding on my sons and my sons' sons.' Then he reached out his hand to take the Sword, and as he did so, a great shout of triumph rose from the ships moored just off the beach. Erik smiled, and his eyes met Thomas's. 'We will not trouble you again.'

Thomas smiled back. 'When my men put to sea, it will not be for the Dalmatic Islands, but to explore to the world's end.'

The islanders and the men of Rossendale returned to the castle together for a great banquet to mark the beginning of the peace. Erik sat at Thomas's right hand, and further down the table sat Billy and Margaret Claypole, full of pride and pleasure, and Dr Castang, already pondering the sentences he would write in the Chronicles. The musicians played and the wine flowed freely. The soldiers drank rowdy toasts to past triumphs, and spoke quietly of the fields they would plough in the spring.

Thomas closed his eyes for a moment and forgot the glad noise and the ceremony and the strangeness of his new life. In his heart he was back in the forest with Luka and Midwinter, and he smiled, knowing he would return.